'Why can't Nick?'

'Because I'm not looking for commitment and never shall be,' he said bluntly, hating to see how she winced. His fingers curled around the cup, because there was no way that he could risk holding her hand again when his emotions were so finely balanced.

'Never is a long time. You might change your mind.'

'I won't. I can't.'

'Can't? What do you mean by that?' Her eyes were luminous with unshed tears and it hurt to know that he was the cause of them.

'Because I made a decision many years ago never to get involved in a long-term relationship and I can't go back on it,' he explained, knowing that he was glossing over the truth.

Jennifer Taylor lives in the north-west of England with her husband Bill. She had been writing Mills & Boon® romances for some years, but when she discovered Medical Romances™ she was so captivated by these heart-warming stories that she set out to write them herself! When not writing or doing research for her latest book, Jennifer's hobbies include reading, travel, walking her dog and retail therapy (shopping!). Jennifer claims all that bending and stretching to reach the shelves is the best exercise possible.

Jennifer Taylor's web page can be viewed at: www.jennifer-taylor.com

Recent titles by the same author:

HIS BROTHER'S SON
LIFE SUPPORT
MORGAN'S SON
THE BABY ISSUE
ADAM'S DAUGHTER
AN ANGEL IN HIS ARMS
THE ITALIAN DOCTOR

A FAMILY OF THEIR OWN

BY
JENNIFER TAYLOR

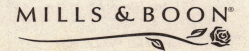

DID YOU PURCHASE THIS BOOK WITHOUT A COVER?

If you did, you should be aware it is **stolen property** as it was reported *unsold and destroyed* by a retailer. Neither the author nor the publisher has received any payment for this book.

All the characters in this book have no existence outside the imagination of the author, and have no relation whatsoever to anyone bearing the same name or names. They are not even distantly inspired by any individual known or unknown to the author, and all the incidents are pure invention.

All Rights Reserved including the right of reproduction in whole or in part in any form. This edition is published by arrangement with Harlequin Enterprises II B.V. The text of this publication or any part thereof may not be reproduced or transmitted in any form or by any means, electronic or mechanical, including photocopying, recording, storage in an information retrieval system, or otherwise, without the written permission of the publisher.

This book is sold subject to the condition that it shall not, by way of trade or otherwise, be lent, resold, hired out or otherwise circulated without the prior consent of the publisher in any form of binding or cover other than that in which it is published and without a similar condition including this condition being imposed on the subsequent purchaser.

MILLS & BOON and MILLS & BOON with the Rose Device are registered trademarks of the publisher.

*First published in Great Britain 2002
Harlequin Mills & Boon Limited,
Eton House, 18-24 Paradise Road, Richmond, Surrey TW9 1SR*

© Jennifer Taylor 2002

ISBN 0 263 83089 6

*Set in Times Roman 10¼ on 11 pt.
03-0902-59679*

*Printed and bound in Spain
by Litografia Rosés, S.A., Barcelona*

CHAPTER ONE

LEANNE RUSSELL had given up a lot to come to London. As she stood in the crowded railway carriage and thought about the decisions she had made, she sighed.

She'd had a good job, a lovely flat *and* she had been on the verge of getting engaged, but she had given it all up without a qualm. She knew that her friends back home in Australia thought she was mad, but they didn't understand.

Discovering that she had been adopted as a baby had shaken the very foundations of her world so that it felt as though she no longer knew who she was any more. She had tried to explain how important it was that she find out the truth about her past, but nobody had understood that, not even Michael—

Especially *not* Michael! she amended swiftly.

Leanne's generous mouth tightened as she thought about the row she'd had with her fiancé, Michael Freeman, shortly before she had left for England. She had hoped that he, at least, would support her decision, but she'd been wrong.

Michael had been furious when she had told him about her plans to go to England. At first she had thought that he'd been concerned about her making the trip on her own, but she couldn't have been more wrong. The only thing that Michael had been worried about had been the fact that the plans he'd made to announce their engagement at the staff Christmas party would have to be changed.

He'd refused to listen when she had tried to explain how important the trip was to her. As he had coldly pointed out, he didn't see why *he* should be inconvenienced because she was setting out on some wild goose chase. In the end, he had cut short the discussion and given her an ultimatum: either stay at home or forget their engagement.

If anything had been guaranteed to prove what a mistake she had made by agreeing to marry him, that had been it. If she was honest, she had already started having doubts about whether Michael was the man she wanted to spend her life with, and the ultimatum had been the last straw. Michael's needs had come first and foremost, and always would. Everyone else's—hers included—had come way down his list of priorities.

The train drew into the station with a hissing of brakes and Leanne snapped out of her reverie. A mechanical voice was announcing that this stop was St Stephen's and to change here for Waterloo and Embankment. She felt her heart give a nervous little jolt as she alighted from the carriage. The first day in her new job was about to begin.

It had been pure good luck that she had happened to find the advertisement on the internet asking for experienced nurses to work at HealthFirst, a medical centre operating out of one of London's busiest railway stations. The jobs were being handled by an Australian recruitment agency, so she had arranged an interview at their office in Sydney.

She had met all HealthFirst's requirements so the agency had emailed her application to London and received a reply, setting up a time when they could telephone and speak to her in person. Five days later she'd signed a three-month contract and faxed it back to their office.

The wonders of modern technology, she thought wryly as she took the escalator up to the station's main concourse. The only problem being that it was a little daunting to be starting a new job without having met any of the people she would be working with.

Would they accept her? she found herself wondering as she stepped off the moving stairway. She had always made friends easily in the past but that had been before she'd found out that she wasn't the person she'd thought herself to be. She wasn't *really* Leanne Russell at all. That had been the name her adoptive parents had given her. Until she found out the truth about herself, she couldn't be certain of anything any more.

Leanne put that unsettling thought to the back of her mind as she crossed the busy concourse. It was a little before eight and the morning rush-hour was under way. She could see the neon sign for HealthFirst glowing above the heads of the commuters. The clinic was on the mezzanine level so she ran up the stairs then paused before opening the door.

She had dressed with extra care that morning, wanting to make a good impression. Although she had been told that a uniform would be provided, it had seemed important that she looked neat and tidy and the black trouser suit and crisp white shirt had seemed the perfect choice.

She was quite tall, a little over five feet nine, with a trim but curvaceous figure, and tailored clothes suited her best. Low-heeled black pumps added a little more to her height and matched the workmanlike leather bag swinging from her shoulder.

She had pinned her collar-length, dark red hair into a French pleat and been sparing with her make-up, relying on a touch of foundation to conceal the sprinkling of freckles that covered her small, straight nose and just a lick of black mascara to emphasise her slate-grey eyes.

Lipstick was something she'd never worn since Michael had told her that it made her mouth look far too big, but just for a moment she found herself wishing that she had worn some that day. It would have helped to bolster her courage if she had been wearing full war-paint, as her mother had always called it.

Thinking about the woman who had brought her up still caused her a lot of pain so she quickly pushed open the door and went inside. There was an attractive blonde woman behind the desk and she looked up with a polite smile.

'Good morning. How may I help you?'

'I'm Leanne Russell, the new practice nurse. I was told to report to Dr Slater,' she explained.

'Oh, hi, there! It's good to meet you, Leanne.' The woman smiled more warmly at her this time. 'I'm Melanie Pickering, another of the nurses here, although my contract runs out in...oh, seventy-one hours and six minutes precisely.'

Leanne laughed. 'Not that you're counting off the minutes, of course. Is it really *that* bad, working here?'

'No way! It's been great and I've really enjoyed it, but it's time to move on.'

Melanie grinned as she got up from behind the desk. 'I'm off to the Philippines next week and I'm really looking forward to it. I've got itchy feet, I'm afraid, so I never stay too long in any one place. Mind you, most of the people who work here are exactly the same. Nick was only saying yesterday that it's like the United Nations in here.'

'Nick?' Leanne prompted, following Melanie down a wide corridor.

The clinic was very modern from what she could see, with lots of chrome and glass and discreetly positioned lighting. They passed an elegantly furnished waiting area and she smiled at a man who was sitting on one of the comfortable chairs, drinking a cup of coffee.

She knew from the literature that had been sent to her that patients attending the clinic paid to see a doctor or a nurse according to a set scale of charges. HealthFirst offered a walk-in service so that people didn't need to make an appointment before they arrived.

'Nick Slater. He's in charge for the next four months while the clinic's director is taking an extended holiday.'

'Another short-term contract,' Leanne observed. They had reached the end of the corridor and Melanie paused outside a door that was standing slightly ajar.

'Most people who work here are employed on a short-term basis. It's one of the main attractions of the job. As for Nick, well, his feet are even itchier than mine! If you've got a couple of hours to spare, ask him to list all the countries he's visited—' She broke off and grimaced when the phone in Reception rang. 'Starting early today from the sound of it. I'll have to leave you and Nick to introduce yourselves. Don't bother knocking. Just go straight in. He's on his own.'

'Thanks,' Leanne murmured as Melanie hurried away. She squared her shoulders then went to open the door when all of a sudden she heard voices coming from inside the room. She paused, realising that Melanie must have been mistaken about Nick Slater being on his own. She would hate to barge in if he had a patient with him...

'Leanne Russell. Aged twenty-four, from Sydney, Australia. Glowing references—highly professional, committed to her work, a credit to her profession, etcetera, etcetera. It all sounds rather too good to be true.'

'Then it probably is.'

Nick Slater tipped back his big leather armchair and placed his booted feet on the edge of the desk. His hazel-green eyes were wry as he looked at the other man. 'If something sounds too good to be true then it usually is in my experience.'

Dennis McNally laughed. 'You're such a cynic, Nick. She could be the real thing, a genuine, bona fide angel.'

'I'll believe that when I see her wings.' Nick chuckled when Dennis groaned. 'Sorry! Bad joke. Anyway, what else do we know about Miss Russell?'

Dennis frowned as he skimmed through the application form. 'Not a lot. She comes from Sydney, as I said, and trained at the Royal Free. She had just been appointed junior sister on the tropical diseases ward—' He broke off when Nick sighed. 'What?'

'Think about it. If you'd just been given a promotion, would you up and leave?' Nick shrugged as he tilted further back in his chair. 'Sounds to me as though Miss Russell might have had another reason for leaving sunny Sydney rather than a simple desire to spend the winter sightseeing in London. Could it have been man trouble, by any chance?

That's just what we need. Someone who's going to spend all her time nursing a broken heart instead of the patients.'

'Come on, Nick,' Dennis protested. 'You don't have any idea why she decided to leave Aus. She might have had a sudden urge to see a bit more of the world. In which case she'll fit in perfectly around here.'

'She might,' Nick replied, not attempting to hide his scepticism. They were under a lot of pressure at HealthFirst and the last thing they needed was a member of the team who didn't pull her weight.

'Well, there's an easy way to test out your theory,' Dennis said cheerfully. 'If Leanne Russell is indeed suffering from a broken heart then she won't be interested in going out on a date, will she? Ask her out and see what kind of a reaction you get.'

'Thanks but, no, thanks.' Nick smiled thinly. 'I'm not in the market for a relationship, especially not with someone who might be on the rebound. The last thing I need is some clinging woman cluttering up my life.'

'Scared she'll turn you down?' Dennis taunted. 'What a blow to the old ego that would be. The great Nick Slater actually getting turned down for a date. That would be a first!'

'There's a first time for everything,' he replied, refusing to rise to the bait, although Dennis's comments had touched a nerve. Was he earning himself a reputation as being a bit of a Lothario, perhaps?

He hoped not. Just because he was careful about avoiding commitment, it didn't mean that he played fast and loose. He was always completely open about his intentions whenever he invited a woman out, made sure that she understood there wasn't any future for the relationship. He had made the decision to remain single after his brother Matt had died, and there was no way that he would risk hurting anyone's feelings by not making his position clear. He had thought that he'd been handling things extremely well, but maybe he had given his colleagues a completely different impression.

He was still pondering on it when he realised that Dennis was speaking. He frowned. 'What did you say?'

'I said I'll bet you a tenner that you can't get Leanne Russell to go out with you,' Dennis repeated obligingly. He grinned when Nick shook his head. 'What are you afraid of? Scared the old Slater charm might not work this time?'

'Of course not,' Nick began, intending to tell Dennis that he had no intention of accepting such a ridiculous challenge—only he never got the chance to finish what he was saying. He felt a frisson run through him when a cool female voice suddenly interrupted their conversation.

'I'd save your money if I were you, Dr Slater.'

Nick looked towards the door and it felt as though he had been punched hard in the solar plexus when he got his first glimpse of the woman who was standing there. In a fascinated sweep his eyes drank in every detail from the glorious, wet-fox red of her hair to the black leather pumps on her narrow feet.

His mind seemed to be awash with impressions all of a sudden, like how smooth her tanned skin looked, how soft her grey eyes seemed to be, how slender her body was under the tailored black suit so that it was a second or two before he realised that she was waiting for him to answer.

It took every scrap of self-possession he could summon to swing his feet from the desk, walk to the door and offer her his hand when he was acutely aware of the predicament he was in. Frankly, it was unforgivable to have been caught discussing her like that.

'It's a pleasure to meet you, Miss Russell,' he said as evenly as he could in the circumstances. 'Welcome to HealthFirst.'

'Thank you.' She placed her hand in his and he barely managed to suppress a shiver when she treated him to a chilly smile.

'However, I think it might be best if I clarify the situation before we go any further. I am neither suffering from a broken heart nor am I looking for a relationship. So if you were thinking of accepting that bet, Dr Slater, I would advise you to change your mind. I would hate you to lose any of your hard-earned cash on my acount.'

Nick knew there must be something he could say to defuse the situation. Usually he was adept at finding the perfect phrase to smooth over the most difficult moment, but the ability seemed to have deserted him all of a sudden.

He took a deep breath as Leanne Russell removed her hand from his because it had just occurred to him why he was having such problems that day. He was *disappointed* because she had stated that she wasn't interested in having a relationship with anyone.

For a man who had spent his whole adult life avoiding any risk of commitment it came as a shock to have to admit it. At that moment he wished that he were anywhere in the world rather than right there in London, facing the biggest test he had ever had to face. Leanne Russell had the power to turn his life upside down if he let her. It was the fact that he couldn't be sure of stopping her that really scared him.

Leanne took a deep breath as she walked into the room, but her heart was hammering. Maybe she could have attributed it to anger because she had been furious when she'd overheard the conversation, but it would be wrong to lie to herself.

The reason her heart was hammering was because she had been holding Nick Slater's hand. Even now she could feel the imprint of his fingers on her skin and had to make a conscious effort not to check her hand for any visible sign. What on earth was the matter with her? Why should she feel like this after what she had overheard him saying?

'It's nice to meet you, Leanne. I'm Dennis McNally, head of the admin staff here at the clinic.'

She jumped when the fair-haired man standing by the desk spoke to her. It was an effort to respond when her mind was whirling, but not for the life of her would she let Nick Slater guess how unsettled she felt.

'Mr McNally,' she replied coolly. He had been the other participant in that conversation and she had no intention of letting him think that he could get away with it. Far better to put an end to any more speculation straight away.

'I hope that you have taken note of what I told Dr Slater, especially the last part of it. I am not in the market for a *relationship*.'

She heard Nick Slater suck in a deep breath when she emphasised that last word and glanced at him. Just for a second their eyes met and held while she felt the oddest sensation run through her. It was as though all the strength had suddenly ebbed from her body. She could feel her arms and legs growing weak, feel her vision starting to blur...

She blinked and the room shot back into focus. Nick Slater had already turned away and she watched as he went to his desk and sat down. He picked up a pen and lined it up with infinite precision along the top edge of his leather-backed blotter.

Leanne bit her lip because she knew with a sudden flash of insight that he was trying to buy himself some time before he had to look at her again. Why? Because he had experienced that same sensation of weakness which had seized her when their eyes had met? It seemed crazy even to think such a thing, yet she knew it was true. And her racing heart raced all the faster.

'I owe you an apology, Miss Russell. Obviously, you weren't meant to overhear what Dennis and I were saying just now, but that is no excuse. It was extremely remiss of us to have been speculating about you that way.'

Nick Slater's deep voice cut through the silence and made her start nervously. Leanne raised startled eyes to his face then quickly looked away because she didn't want to risk making eye contact with him again.

'So long as you both understand that I would take an extremely dim view of you repeating what you said to anyone else, I think we can let the matter drop,' she said, striving for calmness.

'You have my word on it, Miss Russell. Thank you for being so understanding.'

He turned to Dennis McNally and she breathed a sigh of relief at no longer being the object of his interest. 'If you could let me have those figures, Dennis, I can work them into my report. I need to get it faxed to the office this afternoon, so I would appreciate it if you could get straight onto it.'

It was a dismissal and Dennis wasn't slow to see it as such. 'No problem. I'll let you have them before lunch. Nice to meet you, Miss Russell, and, as Nick said, sorry and all that.'

Leanne inclined her head, although she didn't say anything as he hurriedly left the room. She was far too busy worrying about being alone with Nick Slater to think about anything else. It stunned her that she should be so aware of him because it had never happened before, not even when she had met Michael.

That thought was less than comforting so it was a relief when Nick briskly stood up and walked to the door. 'I'll give you a quick tour of the place first. I'm afraid that you're getting thrown in at the deep end because we are short-staffed at the moment.'

'Show me any medical facility that isn't short of staff,' she said lightly, following him into the corridor.

She took a steadying breath as he locked his office door. If she focused solely on the job and stopped her mind from running off at tangents, it would help tremendously.

'You're obviously a realist. Good. The last nurse we hired only lasted a week. She had got it into her head that life would be easier working in a place where the patients didn't have their treatment provided by the NHS, with all its attendant problems.'

He gave a deep laugh and Leanne held herself rigid when she felt a spasm shoot through her again. 'Unfortunately, it has just the opposite effect. Because people pay for their treatment they expect a much better service. Woe betide you if you don't come up to their expectations!'

'It's only natural, I suppose.'

She cleared her throat when she heard how husky her voice had sounded. She had to stop this, she told herself sternly. Had to stop reacting to everything Nick Slater said or did. He was just someone she would be working with for the next three months so maybe she should slot him into that category right away.

'People expect value for money,' she continued in a more normal tone. 'It doesn't matter if they're buying a new car, groceries from the supermarket or medical care, they expect the very best for their hard-earned money.'

'Exactly. And that's what we aim to give them when they come to HealthFirst,' Nick assured her. 'Our aim is to provide a comprehensive, value-for-money service to all our patients.'

'Do you deal mainly with minor ailments?' she asked curiously.

'Not at all. We provide the full range of services that any general practitioner would offer. If we see a patient and decide that he needs a hospital referral—we arrange it. We also offer a complete range of diagnostic tests—blood, urine, cholesterol, electrocardiograph, and so on. And we refer any which are beyond our scope to a specialist provider.'

'Are the people you treat usually holidaymakers?' she said, a little surprised by the extent of the services on offer at the clinic.

'No, again.' He paused and she steeled herself when she realised that he was looking at her. She knew that she couldn't keep avoiding making eye contact with him, but it was difficult to make herself turn and face him.

It was a relief when she felt nothing but the tiniest tremor as their eyes met, and that could easily be attributed to first-day nerves. Maybe that also helped to explain what had happened before? she mused. After all, it wasn't as though Nick

Slater was the best-looking man she had ever seen, was he? She made herself take stock, bit by bit, hoping that it would help to work this glitch out of her system if she saw him simply as the person he was.

His hair was dark brown and cut very short because she guessed that it had a tendency to curl if he let it grow. His eyes were hazel rather than the pure green she had first thought them to be, heavily lashed with thick, straight, black lashes. His nose had a definite crook in it, as though it might have been broken on more than one occasion, possibly playing some kind of sport. He definitely had an athlete's physique with those broad shoulders and that well-muscled chest, the trim waist and narrow hips...

Leanne paused when she realised that she'd allowed herself to be sidetracked and had skipped a bit. Her gaze backtracked while she took note of a mobile mouth that naturally curved up at the corners, a strong chin with just the hint of a dimple in it, a pair of well-shaped ears.

All in all, Nick Slater was a nice-looking man in his thirties, not exactly heart-throb material but verging on it, she decided. She could understand a woman being attracted to him and it was a comfort to realise that. But was it *really* enough to help explain how she had reacted to him?

She tried to tell herself that it was possible—*probable* even if it was added to the understandable nervousness of starting a new job—but she wasn't convinced. The way she had responded to Nick Slater wasn't going to be explained away that easily.

Nick cleared his throat purely and simply because he wasn't sure what else to do. Leanne was staring at him and it made him feel very odd to be on the receiving end of such an intent scrutiny. 'Over half of the people whom we see at HealthFirst are UK citizens.'

He coughed again, wondering what was wrong with his vocal cords. His voice had the quavery cadence of a teenage boy. In fact, now that he thought about it, he felt rather like he had done as a teenager when he'd developed a crush on the school's gym mistress...

This time his cough was genuine and he saw Leanne look at him in concern. 'Are you OK?'

'Fine.' He managed to suck some air into his lungs but it was an effort to act as though there was nothing wrong. How in the name of all that was holy had he developed a *crush* on Leanne Russell in the space of ten minutes?

'Just a tickle in my throat. What was I saying...? Oh, yes, most of the patients we treat here are business people who can't get to see their own GPs because the surgeries' hours don't correspond with their busy schedules. They appreciate the fact that they can call into the clinic and be seen virtually straight away.'

'And they are prepared to pay for this service?' she queried, frowning.

'Yes.' Nick shrugged, striving for a nonchalance he wished he felt. Of course he hadn't developed a crush on Leanne—the idea was ridiculous. But, try as he may, he couldn't dismiss it.

'You know the old saying that time is money? Well, it applies in this instance. People don't have the time to hang around a GP's surgery when they should be at work. We aim never to have any patient wait longer than fifteen minutes even during our busiest periods, which are the morning and evening rush hours. And most are seen well before then.'

'You must have a big staff working here with targets like that?'

'We have thirty people employed here at the present time and we are currently advertising five more vacancies.' He smiled when he saw her surprise then found himself wondering if she realised how expressive her face was. Everything she thought showed. He'd noticed that before when she'd been staring at him...

He shut off the rest of that thought. To recall the bewilderment he had seen in Leanne's expressive grey eyes certainly wouldn't help. Maybe she was having trouble understanding this *awareness* they both seemed to feel, but letting himself get hung up on the idea would cause even more problems.

'We're open from eight in the morning to eight at night, seven days a week,' he explained, steadfastly confining his thoughts to work. 'That's a lot of hours to cover, especially when a number of the staff working here are only employed on a part-time basis.'

'Like me. I decided that full-time work would be too constricting which is why I opted to do twenty-five hours a week when I accepted the job. I was worried that I wouldn't have enough free time if I did more than that.'

Nick frowned because he wasn't sure what she had meant. 'Enough time to go sightseeing, you mean?'

'No. I didn't come to London to go sightseeing. I…well, I had another reason for coming.'

She didn't elaborate, leaving him with the distinct impression that she didn't want him to question her further. All of a sudden that conversation he'd had with Dennis came flooding back, but with a new twist.

Had Leanne come to London on her own, as they had assumed, or was she here with someone else, maybe her boyfriend? She had said that she wasn't suffering from a broken heart or looking for a relationship so it seemed to fit. And maybe she had chosen to work part time so that she could spend more time with him.

Nick took a deep breath. He knew that he really should stop all this speculating. Leanne's reasons for coming to London had nothing whatsoever to do with him. His only concern was making sure that she did her job properly, yet he knew in his heart how difficult it was going to be to stick to that. The thought of Leanne and some unknown man spending their time together made him feel all knotted up inside. Although he hated to admit it, he knew why.

He was *jealous* at the thought of her being with another

man, at the idea of her spending time with someone who wasn't him.

Hell and damnation! That was something he certainly hadn't bargained for.

CHAPTER TWO

'IF YOU could just wait a moment...'

Leanne bit back a sigh when she saw the lack of comprehension on the young woman's face. So far all she had managed to establish was that the patient's name was Chantal Dupré and that she was from Paris. Why Chantal needed to see a doctor was something she still had to find out.

Dredging her mind, Leanne summoned up a few words of school French. *'Un moment, s'il vous plait, mademoiselle.'*

Leaving the young woman sitting in Reception, she hurried off in search of Melanie, hoping that she might be able to help her solve the problem. After Nick Slater had finished giving her a tour of the clinic, he had asked her if she would take over the reception duties.

She'd been a little surprised by the request until he had explained that it helped to have someone medically trained greeting the patients on their arrival, to act as triage nurse. Minor ailments could be passed to one of the nursing staff, more serious matters referred to a doctor and any urgent cases could be rushed straight through.

It had been a gentle introduction to the work carried out at the clinic and she'd rather enjoyed it until she had encountered the problem of a patient who spoke no English. She spotted Melanie coming out of one of the treatment rooms and greeted her with relief.

'How's your French? I've got a woman in Reception who doesn't speak any English and I'm stuck.'

'Nick's your man. He speaks French, Spanish, Italian, plus a smattering of umpteen other languages,' Melanie told her cheerfully. 'He's in his office so give him a shout.'

'Thanks,' Leanne murmured as Melanie escorted her patient out. She made her way to Nick's office and knocked on the door, refusing to think about what had happened a couple of hours earlier. Actually getting down to some work had helped enormously to calm her nerves, although she had to confess to a sudden attack of the jitters when she heard Nick inviting her in. She bit back a sigh. Whichever way she looked at it, her reaction to Nick Slater was very strange.

It was hardly the most comforting of thoughts so she did her best to put it out of her mind as she entered the room. Nick was at his desk and he looked up with an abstracted smile.

'Problems?'

'Kind of. I have a Frenchwoman in Reception who doesn't speak any English. Melanie said that you speak French…'

'So you want me to translate for you?' He took off the rimless glasses he was wearing and tossed them on the desk then grinned at her. 'It will be a pleasure. Anything to get away from this wretched paperwork!'

Leanne laughed softly but she couldn't deny that her heart had given an uncomfortable little thump when he had smiled at her. 'You'd think things would have got easier since computers came on the scene, but it hasn't made much difference, I've found.'

'You and me both,' he agreed, easing himself out of the chair and groaning. 'I've only been working on this wretched report for a couple of hours but it feels like a lifetime. If there's one thing I hate, it's being stuck behind a desk.'

'One of the hazards of the job, I would have thought,' she observed. 'Most GPs end up spending a lot of their time desk-bound.'

'Which is yet another reason why I'm glad that I decided not to join the family firm,' he responded, making for the door.

Leanne frowned as she followed him into the corridor. 'Family firm? What do you mean?'

'My mother and father are both GPs, although Mum only works a couple of days a week now, covering the post- and antenatal clinics. My older brother Patrick works with them and my sister Helen was the practice nurse at the surgery until she had her youngest child and found it was too much for her. Benjie is her fourth,' he explained dryly. 'So I think she deserves a bit of time off, don't you?'

'I most certainly do,' she exclaimed. 'Four children are a lot to cope with. But it's amazing that your whole family works together like that. It must be marvellous for them.'

'Depends on what you want from life, I suppose,' he said shortly.

Leanne looked at him curiously. 'Meaning that it isn't what you want?'

'No. I have no intention of spending the rest of my life stuck in Sussex. There's too much of the world I haven't seen yet.'

'You'll have to settle down one day,' she protested.

'Why? There's no rule that says you have to stay put in one place.'

His tone was harsh and she had the feeling that he was annoyed, but why? Because of what she'd said or because of something that had happened in his past?

She had no time to work it out, however, because they had arrived at Reception by then. Nick went straight to the young Frenchwoman and briefly conferred with her then drew Leanne forward.

'Mademoiselle Dupré needs emergency contraception. Can you deal with it?'

'Of course,' she agreed at once. 'How long ago was it that she had unprotected sex?'

'Last night so there shouldn't be a problem. As you know, the tablets need to be taken within seventy-two hours of intercourse taking place.'

He glanced round when the door opened and another patient came in. 'Why don't you take Mademoiselle Dupré into one of the treatment rooms and fill in all the details on her card? I'll leave it to you to administer the drugs. You can sign for them at the pharmacy.

'I'll have another word with her before she leaves and make sure that she understands what she has to do. Melanie can take over the desk again now that she's finished with her patient.'

'Fine,' Leanne agreed immediately. She smiled at the young Frenchwoman, signalling that she should follow her. Opening the door to one of the immaculately furnished treatment rooms, she indicated that Chantal should wait there while she fetched the medication.

Emergency contraception—commonly called the morning-after pill—consisted of two high-dose oral contraceptive pills taken as soon as possible after intercourse. They were followed twelve hours later by a further two pills. Although the treatment wasn't one hundred per cent guaranteed to work, it was effective in most cases.

Nick would explain to Chantal Dupré that, if she missed her next period, she would need to take a pregnancy test in a month's time, just to be certain, Leanne thought as she signed for the tablets. The poor woman obviously wouldn't be pleased to discover that she was pregnant after she had taken steps to avoid it.

She sighed as she made her way back to the treatment room. Had her own birth mother been dismayed when she had found out that she was pregnant? She must have been otherwise she would never have given her daughter up for adoption.

It made Leanne wonder if her friends had been right and if she was making a mistake by trying to track down the woman who had given her away. After all, her adoptive parents had given her all the love she could possibly have needed, so was it wise to go raking up the past when she might be disappointed by what she discovered? Maybe she had always longed for brothers and sisters, aunts, uncles and cousins, but there was no guarantee that she would have much in common with them if she did find them. Nick had obviously made a conscious decision to escape the ties of his family.

That thought made her frown. Maybe she was reading too much into the situation, but she had a feeling that there was a reason why he had cut himself off like that and that it hadn't been just a desire to travel either. What had happened to make Nick decide to leave his family?

For some reason it seemed important that she find out.

'Merci, mademoiselle. Au revoir.'

Nick closed the door after Chantal Dupré finally left then glanced at his watch. The woman had been so delighted to find someone who could understand her that she had kept him talking. He was very aware that the report he needed to submit was lying on his desk, half-finished. Even though he loathed paperwork, he usually got down to it, but it seemed to be taking an inordinate amount of time that day. The trouble was that his mind kept skipping off at tangents all the time.

He squared his shoulders, refusing to let himself be sidetracked again. He had spent enough time thinking about Leanne Russell for one day. He hurried back to his office but he had barely sat down when there was a knock on the door and Robert Ashford, one of the duty doctors, poked his head into the room.

'Sorry to bother you, Nick, but I've got a guy with me I'd like you to take a look at.'

'What's the problem?' he asked, immediately getting up.

Robert was from Tennessee and he was spending six months in the UK before he took up a residency at a hospital in his home town. Nick had found him to be extremely competent and didn't doubt that there was a genuine problem if Robert had seen fit to ask for his opinion.

'It's very vague—fever, lassitude, quite noticeable enlargement of the glands in his neck.' Robert shrugged. 'He's obviously unwell, there's no doubt about that, but I can't put my finger on the problem.'

'Have you ordered blood tests?' Nick asked, accompanying him from the room.

'Yessiree. I'm waiting on the lab. They've promised to get back to me a.s.a.p. I just thought it might help if you had a look in case I've missed something,' Robert replied laconically.

Nick nodded. 'Fine by me.'

He followed the younger man into one of the treatment rooms and introduced himself to the patient. 'I'm Nick Slater, acting head of the clinic. Dr Ashford has asked me to take a look at you.'

'Take as many as you like,' the middle-aged man replied, making an obvious effort to sound cheerful. 'If you can work out what's wrong with me, I'll be eternally grateful. I've felt like hell these past few days, I can tell you.'

Nick smiled as he picked up the chart Robert had filled in. 'We shall give it our best shot. It's Mr Jacobs, is it, and you work for the Foreign Office?'

'That's right. Been with them for twenty years now. I've been working on overseas aid and development for the past three,' Ian Jacobs replied.

'Really? That must be interesting. Do you get to go overseas a lot, or is it mainly a desk job?' Nick carefully checked the man's neck. He nodded to Robert when he felt how enlarged the glands were.

'A bit of both, actually. I've been to quite a lot of places in the past few years—India, Africa, places like that.'

'And were you ever ill when you were away on any of these trips?' Nick asked, trying to get a full picture of what might be wrong with the man.

'Not that I can remember...' Ian Jacobs frowned. 'A bit of a tummy upset in India, but several members of the party suffered with it, as I recall. The sanitation where we were staying left a lot to be desired.'

'That's the problem with so many of these Third World

countries,' he observed lightly. 'Anything else? Were you bitten by a dog, scratched by a cat, made a meal of by mosquitoes?'

Ian laughed ruefully. 'The mosquitoes had a field day with me! I was covered in bites most of the time. But I was very careful about taking precautions, Dr Slater. I was on antimalarial tablets throughout each trip and continued using them after I came home as per instructions. Do you think it's possible that I might have contracted malaria?'

Nick shook his head when he heard the worry in the man's voice. 'Not if you took the medication exactly as you were advised to do. Most modern antimalaria treatment is effective. I assume that you used the ones best suited to the countries you were visiting? There are different strains of malaria so any preventative medicine must take account of that.'

'Oh, yes. We were given the most up-to-date information before we travelled. One thing the Foreign Office is good at is looking after their employees when they are in the field,' Ian Jacobs assured him.

'That's good to hear. Now, just to recap. Dr Ashford told me that you've been suffering from bouts of fever; is that right?'

'Yes. I can't recall ever experiencing anything like it, not even when I came down with flu several years ago. And I feel so worn out all the time, as though I can barely make the effort to do anything,' the man confessed.

'I see. And there's nothing else at all that you can add? Something quite insignificant, perhaps.' Nick smiled reassuringly but he was as puzzled as Robert was about the case. 'We work a bit like Sherlock Holmes—if we eliminate the possible and find ourselves left with the improbable, then it is quite often the answer.'

'Well, there's an insect bite which has been a bit of a nuisance... But I really can't see that it's the cause of how ill I've been feeling.'

'Let's take a look. It would be silly not to check it out,

wouldn't it?' Nick bit back a sigh. It never failed to amaze him how reluctant people were to impart information.

'It's here on my hip.' Ian pulled down his underwear so that Nick could see the small lump on his hip. 'It's quite painful, actually. So much so that I find myself lying on my other side at night in bed.'

Nick gently probed the nodule, murmuring an apology when he felt Ian wince. He glanced at Robert and raised his brows. 'What do you think?'

'I'm not sure, but it doesn't look like any mosquito bite that I've ever seen,' the younger doctor told him doubtfully.

'Exactly what I thought. If I'm not mistaken, it's a tsetse fly bite.' He glanced at the patient again. 'Which part of Africa did you visit and how long ago were you there?'

'We were on the west coast about a month ago. Doesn't the tsetse fly carry sleeping sickness?'

'That's right.' He patted Ian Jacobs's shoulder when he heard the alarm in his voice. 'However, even if I'm right—and we'll need the results of the blood tests to confirm that—then sleeping sickness is curable if you catch it early enough. As soon as we can establish if that is what's wrong with you, you will be started on a course of drugs to kill the parasites that have got into your bloodstream.'

He paused as a thought occurred to him. Leanne had worked on the tropical diseases ward of the Sydney hospital so maybe she could help to confirm his diagnosis? Obviously, his sole reason for involving her was the patient's welfare, he told himself quickly when alarm bells started to ring inside his head. It had nothing whatsoever to do with the fact that he wanted to see her again.

'We have a new nurse working here who was a sister on the tropical diseases ward at the Royal Free Hospital in Sydney,' he explained before he thought better of it. 'Would you mind if I asked her to take a look, Mr Jacobs?'

'Not at all,' the man said quickly. 'The sooner you establish what this is, then the faster I can be treated.'

'Exactly.' Nick excused himself and left the room. He

made his way to Reception but Melanie was behind the desk. She looked up when he appeared.

'Did you want me, Nick?'

'I was looking for Leanne, actually,' he explained, trying to quell the shiver that ran through him when he said her name. It was so ridiculous for a grown man of thirty-five to be acting that way that his mouth compressed and he saw Melanie frown in concern.

'There's nothing wrong, is there? Leanne hasn't done anything to upset you?'

'Of course not.' He fixed a smile to his mouth but it was an effort to hold it in place. Get a grip, Slater! he told himself sternly. Stop acting like a moron and start acting like a doctor.

It was good advice but as he made his way to the supply room, where Leanne was checking in a delivery, he knew how difficult it was going to be to follow it. Leanne and being sensible were two concepts his mind had difficulty putting together. He didn't want to act like a doctor when she was around. He wanted to act like a man in the company of a woman whom he found overwhelmingly attractive.

Leanne ticked off the last item on the list and slipped the delivery note into her pocket. She took a quick look around the small room to make sure that everything was where it was meant to be. Her eyes alighted on half a dozen boxes of hypodermic syringes which she had put on the floor while she'd unpacked the rest of the delivery and she sighed. They needed putting away before she finished.

She quickly pulled over the ladder so that she could put the boxes in their rightful place on the top shelf. She was halfway up the steps when she heard someone coming into the room and automatically glanced round to see who it was. Her foot missed the rung she had been aiming for when she found herself looking into a familiar pair of hazel-green eyes.

'Careful!' Nick made a grab for her as she swayed perilously, his hands clamping firmly on her hips while he steadied her.

Leanne sucked in a little breath through lips that felt as though they had turned to rubber all of a sudden. She could feel the warmth of his palms against her hip bones, feel his fingers curving around the lower part of her abdomen, and the sensations that were flowing through her at that moment weren't ones she should have been feeling about a man she had known barely three hours. All of a sudden, she was awash with desire to feel his hands on other parts of her body, to feel them caressing her and bringing alive the passion that was simmering inside her...

'Are you OK? Do you want me to help you down if you're feeling dizzy?'

She blinked when he spoke, feeling her face suffuse with heat when she realised that she had been standing there, daydreaming about Nick making love to her. Frankly, it was a scenario guaranteed to give her sleepless nights for weeks to come, but she couldn't afford to worry about that right then.

'No, I'm fine.'

She swiftly deposited the boxes on the shelf, murmuring her thanks like an obedient child when he handed her the rest of them. He stepped back as she began to descend and she had to physically stop herself flinching when he put a steadying hand under her elbow as she stepped off the bottom rung.

'You need to be careful in here,' he said in a tone that made her heart bump. 'It would be easy to fall and hurt yourself.'

'Especially when you aren't watching what you're doing,' she replied, trying to inject a little levity into her voice.

She shot him a wary glance as they left the room, but it was hard to decide why he had sounded so edgy. Maybe he'd been worried about what would have happened if she'd fallen off the ladder? After all, it wouldn't reflect well on him if a new employee ended up injuring herself on her first day in the job.

Funnily enough that idea stung, but she forced herself to ignore it when he turned to her. 'I wonder if you would mind taking a look at a patient for me?'

'Me?' she exclaimed, not attempting to hide her surprise.

'Yes, you.' Nick grinned. 'Don't be so modest. You wouldn't have been hired for this job if you weren't good at what you do.'

'Why, thank you, Dr Slater. I'm completely overwhelmed.' She smiled back, unable to resist the warm amusement in his eyes.

'So you should be. I don't hand out compliments like that every day of the week,' he retorted, leading the way along the corridor.

'In other words, you're soft-soaping me because you want a favour?'

'Something like that.' He gave her a last smile then made an obvious effort to concentrate on what he needed to tell her. And it was the fact that it *was* such an effort that made Leanne's heart race.

She wasn't a complete innocent and knew that men found her attractive. She had dated her fair share back home in Australia before she'd met Michael. She had believed at first that what she'd felt for Michael had been the embodiment of everything she'd ever wanted, but she'd been wrong. She knew that now when she looked at Nick, because he made her feel things no other man had made her feel.

All of a sudden she was overcome by sadness that she should have met him when her life was in such a state of flux. Until she found out about the mother who had abandoned her, she wasn't in a position to start a relationship, not that Nick would be interested, of course. She had heard what he'd said that morning about not wanting a woman cluttering up his life, so it would be silly to imagine that he was looking for commitment.

It should have made it easier to know that he felt the same

way she did, but it didn't. It felt as though there was a big gap in her life, one that might never be filled. Knowing that you couldn't have something, it didn't stop you wanting it. It didn't stop her wanting Nick.

'This is Leanne Russell. Would you mind if she takes a look at that lump on your hip, Mr Jacobs?'

Nick moved aside as the patient readily gave his permission. It was rather crowded in the room with three of them gathered around the bed. He felt Leanne's arm brush his as she stepped forward, and gritted his teeth when a spasm shot through him.

He had just about managed to damp down the desire he'd felt when he'd steadied her on that ladder. However, once again he felt his body surge to life and had to swallow a groan of dismay. What was it about her that seemed to push all the right buttons or, rather, all the wrong ones?

He wasn't interested in commitment, he couldn't be. How could he commit himself to a woman when he had nothing to offer her? It had been hard to accept that he should remain single all his life, but it had been the right decision. He couldn't take the risk of letting himself fall in love, *wouldn't* take the risk of breaking anyone's heart. Love, marriage and commitment led to children, and children were the one thing he couldn't have.

He knew how he had to live his life, but it made not a scrap of difference in this instance. When he looked at Leanne, when he touched her, common sense deserted him. All he could think about was how much he wanted her...

'I've seen this type of insect bite on a number of occasions.'

Nick jolted back to the present, feeling a little colour run up his cheeks when he found her watching him. He could only pray that he wasn't quite so open about his feelings as she was because he'd had a pretty good idea what she'd been thinking in the supply room.

'You have?' He cleared his throat when he heard how

rough his voice sounded. He couldn't afford to think about that now, but it was hard not to. Knowing that Leanne had wanted him as well gave him hot and cold chills. 'You're sure about that?'

'Quite sure. It's a tsetse fly bite.' She turned to the patient and smiled. 'I take it that you didn't get this in London, Mr Jacobs?'

'I most certainly didn't,' Ian Jacobs replied with a laugh.

Nick held himself rigid when he saw the appreciation in the older man's eyes as he looked at Leanne. There was no way that he would allow himself to feel jealous! But telling himself that didn't seem to make a scrap of difference.

'So you were in Africa, I take it? Which part?' she continued.

'On the west coast.' Ian Jacobs frowned. 'Why did you both ask me that? Isn't the disease prevalent all over the continent?'

'Yes, it is, but there are two different forms of trypanosomiasis, or sleeping sickness as it's more commonly called,' she explained. 'The strain which is found in the east of the continent mainly affects cattle, although it can be transmitted to people. It's a far more aggressive strain and develops in weeks rather than months. You may find this hard to believe, but if it is sleeping sickness, you're lucky that you caught it in the west.'

'Really?' Ian sounded shocked. 'Exactly how much damage can it cause? I've heard about it, of course, but I'm rather vague as to the details.'

Nick took over then when Leanne glanced at him. He guessed that she wanted him to decide how much to tell the man. They weren't in the business of lying to people, but it would be wrong to scare him.

'The west and central strain of the disease is fairly slow running. Once the parasites have got into your bloodstream then it can take months or even years for the disease to develop fully. Fortunately, you will be receiving treatment immediately so that won't be a problem. The heart and the brain are both severely affected if sleeping sickness is allowed to run its course, but it can be cured with the right combination of drugs.'

'There's no chance of it having affected my heart and brain, is there?' Ian demanded, anxiously.

'It's most unlikely at this early stage,' Nick assured him. He glanced at Leanne. 'How did the patients you treated fare?'

'They made full recoveries,' she said immediately, but he could tell that she was glossing over the facts. Although it was true that a cure could be effected with the right drugs, they were known to have unpleasant side-effects. Obviously, Leanne knew that but didn't want to worry the patient by telling him so.

He sighed because it brought it home to him once again how aware of her he was. Robert didn't appear to have noticed that she'd been somewhat economical with the truth and neither had Ian.

She excused herself soon afterwards and Nick concentrated on explaining to Ian what would happen next. The man would be referred to a specialist at a nearby hospital, who would be able to start him on the most appropriate form of treatment.

Ian was eager to make the appointment that day so Nick went to his office and put through a call. It all took some time, plus a little gentle persuasion on his part, but eventually everything was arranged. Ian was despatched by taxi to the hospital.

It was lunchtime by then, but Nick didn't bother going out for anything to eat. He still had the report to finish and he would be hard-pressed to get it done on time. He looked up when he heard footsteps pausing outside his door and felt his heart perform the strangest manoeuvre when he saw Leanne in the doorway. It was an effort to act as though there was nothing wrong when it felt as though his pulse was trying for a new Olympic record.

'Are you off now?'

'Yes. I'll see you tomorrow.' She started to leave, stopped, glanced back then shrugged. 'Bye.'

'Bye,' he repeated, because it was easier than thinking up anything more witty.

He took a deep breath as she hurried away and held it for a count of ten. It didn't help. His pulse was still hammering at high speed. Whichever way he looked at it, working with Leanne was going to be a challenge.

CHAPTER THREE

LEANNE was up before six the following morning. She hadn't slept well and it had seemed easier to get up rather than lie in bed, staring at the ceiling.

She had spent the previous afternoon trying to find out more about her mother. According to her birth certificate, the woman's name was Mary Calhoun. However, when Leanne had tried to find the address that was given on the certificate, she had drawn a blank. The street where her mother had lived had been demolished and there was now a supermarket on the site.

It was rather depressing to have come up against an obstacle at such an early stage, but she tried not to let it get her down as she showered and dressed in her new uniform. She made herself some coffee and toast then set off for work even though it was really too early to leave. She would just have to wait if there was nobody at the clinic to let her in.

She'd found a poky little flat close to Euston station when she'd arrived in London so she didn't have far to walk to catch the tube. The weather was grey and dreary, gusts of rain sweeping along the street. As she joined the long line of commuters waiting to get on the escalators she found herself thinking wistfully about the weather back home in Sydney. At this time of the year—early November—the days would be hot and sunny.

'Fancy running into you. I didn't realise you lived round here.'

She jumped when a familiar voice suddenly spoke in her ear. She felt her heart jolt when she turned and found Nick walking alongside her. She had carefully attributed her sleeplessness to disappointment at not having made any headway in her efforts to trace her mother, but it wasn't as easy to lie to herself when Nick was standing right there beside her. More than once she'd found her thoughts returning to him during the night and at one point, when she'd dropped off to sleep, it had been Nick she'd been dreaming about.

'What are you doing here?' she exclaimed, feeling herself blush. She could scarcely believe that she'd had such erotic dreams about someone who was a virtual stranger to her. She couldn't recall *ever* dreaming about Michael that way.

It was an unsettling thought and she hurried on. 'Silly question! Obviously you're doing the same as me and catching the tube to work.'

'Got it in one!' Nick laughed as he stepped onto the escalator then turned to face her. 'So, whereabout do you live, then?'

Leanne willed her racing heart to calm down, but it wasn't easy to control it. It didn't help that Nick was standing on the step below her so that they were on eye level. She found herself suddenly entranced by the green flecks in his velvety brown eyes, by the way his thick, black lashes cast shadows onto his cheeks. It was an effort to focus on the question he'd asked her.

'Penkworth Street. I'm renting a flat there, well, if you can call one tiny room with a sofa bed and a cupboard for a kitchen a flat.'

'It's amazing what passes for a flat in London.' He smiled ruefully. 'I've not yet decided if estate agents are actually dishonest or if they suffer from rose-tinted-spectacle syndrome. Maybe it *is* an illness which makes them describe ten square feet of living space in such glowing terms.'

Leanne laughed. 'I think you are being far too kind. And if you saw my *flat*, you would most certainly agree with me!'

'Ditto my own less than salubrious accommodation,' he replied easily.

The escalator reached the bottom and he paused to wait

for her. Leanne shivered when he put a steadying hand under her elbow as she stepped off.

His manners were impeccable, she thought as he led the way to the next in the series of escalators which would carry them down into the bowels of the underground railway system. Michael had never bothered opening doors for her or helping her off escalators so she appreciated the small courtesies all the more, then wondered why she kept comparing the two men all the time.

Nick was just a colleague whereas Michael had been her fiancé. It was silly to keep weighing up one against the other and alarming to discover that Nick kept coming out on top.

'So where do you live?' she said quickly, not wanting to go any further along that avenue.

'Sandwell Gardens.' Once again he turned to face her and grinned. 'And before you get the wrong idea, the name sounds far grander than the actual place is! The said gardens boil down to a scrubby bit of grass and a few pathetic trees.'

'But at least you do have grass and trees,' she said tartly. 'The only thing I can see from my window are the houses across the road. The view is less than inspiring, I assure you.'

'In other words, count my blessings, eh?'

His gaze was warm, far warmer than it should have been bearing in mind the short time they'd known one another. Yet it didn't feel as though it had only been a matter of hours since she'd met him, she realised. It felt as though she'd known him for ever. Maybe she had in a way because Nick was the living, breathing embodiment of the man she'd always dreamed of spending her life with.

The thought shocked her so much that she gasped, and she saw his eyes darken with concern. 'Are you all right?'

'Yes, fine.' She hunted for an explanation because telling him the truth was out of the question. Nick would run a mile if he found out that she'd decided he was the blueprint of the man she had always wanted to marry.

'I just remembered that I meant to phone my father last

night,' she said, using the first excuse she could think of. 'I promised to let him know how my first day at work had gone and it completely slipped my mind.'

'He's probably worried sick that you've been abducted by slave traders,' Nick said lightly, but she was relieved to see that he seemed to have accepted her story.

They reached the platform and Leanne followed as he made his way through the crowds of people who were waiting for the next train to arrive. He turned to her when they reached a relatively quiet spot.

'Why don't you phone him from the clinic? You can always reimburse the company for the call so it isn't a problem. I know what my dad is like when my sisters are away—he worries himself to death in case something has happened to them.'

'No, it's OK. I'll do it tonight,' she assured him, then frowned as she mulled over what he'd said. 'I thought you had just the one sister, the one who was a nurse at your parents' practice.'

'I've a younger sister as well. Penny is the baby of the family. She's just been accepted as a junior houseman at Bart's. She's also getting married in two weeks' time, which is why I came back to England.'

'You are lucky!' she exclaimed wistfully. 'I can't imagine what it must be like, being part of a big family like that. I always longed to have brothers and sisters.'

'It has its ups and downs. It isn't all good.'

'What do you mean?' She looked at him curiously, unable to ignore the pain she had heard in his voice. Without stopping to think, she laid her hand on his arm. 'Nick, tell me.'

She heard him take a deep breath and when he spoke she felt her eyes prickle with tears because of the sadness in his voice. 'I had another brother as well—my twin, Matt. He died when he was twenty-six.'

'I am *so* sorry! I don't know what to say apart from that…' She felt her throat clog up with emotion and turned away because she didn't want him to see how much it had upset her. She couldn't begin to imagine how it must feel to lose someone as close to you as a twin brother.

Their train arrived just then and in the scramble to squeeze into the carriage there was no chance to say anything else. Nick stood beside her as the train roared through the tunnel. They were packed so tightly together that she could feel the heat from his body all down her side, but she didn't try to move away.

Maybe it would help to lessen his grief if he knew she was there for him, she thought wistfully. She might be reading too much into a situation she knew very little about, but she sensed that his brother's death still affected Nick. If there was any way that she could help him, she would do so. It might be only hours since they had met but she cared about this man. She really did.

Nick was glad when the journey was over. Standing so close to Leanne in the crowded carriage had been a test of endurance he could have done without. Talking about Matt's death always upset him, but it wasn't only thoughts of his brother which had plagued him.

Every time the carriage had swayed, he had felt Leanne's breast pressing against his arm, her thigh making the most fleeting yet tantalising contact with his own. Frankly, he was a bundle of nerves by the time they reached St Stephen's station and couldn't wait to alight. Being that close to Leanne had tested his self-control beyond any reasonable limits, but he couldn't afford to forget the rules by which he'd lived for the past ten years.

It was a depressing thought but he tried not to show how much it upset him as they stepped off the escalator into the station's concourse. Nick paused and looked round, wondering what he should do. He had left home early with the express intention of having breakfast at one of the station's numerous cafés, and it had suddenly occurred to him how rude it would be not to invite Leanne along.

'I was going to stop for coffee and something to eat,' he

explained, turning to her. He felt his heart bump painfully when she looked around and he saw the concern in her beautiful grey eyes.

Had she guessed how upset he always felt whenever he spoke about Matt? he thought wonderingly. Was that why she looked so sad all of a sudden, because she cared that he was hurting?

He sensed it was so and it was both a pleasure and a pain to realise it because he couldn't afford to wallow in the comfort she could offer him. He had to stick to the decision he'd made all those years ago. He could never ask a woman to commit herself to him when he had nothing to offer her.

'How do you fancy joining me for breakfast? My treat.' It was an effort to behave naturally when his mind was suddenly awash with desires which he had thought he'd put behind him a long time ago.

'Oh, that's very kind—' she began, and he found himself interrupting when he sensed that she was going to refuse. Maybe he *was* playing with fire, but the thought of spending a little more time on his own with her was too tempting to resist.

'Say that you'll come,' he coaxed. 'Just a quick cup of coffee and maybe a roll if you're not very hungry? I hate eating on my own so you will be doing me a favour.' He smiled appealingly at her, watching the rapid play of emotions that crossed her face before she shrugged.

'Why not? A cup of coffee might help to warm me up.' She gave an exaggerated shiver. 'I still haven't acclimatised to the British weather.'

'Even we British haven't acclimatised to our weather, which is why it's such an endlessly fascinating topic of conversation!'

He quirked a brow when she chuckled, trying to disguise how pleased he felt that she had accepted his invitation. Frankly, he couldn't understand why it should mean so much to him. All they were going to do was share coffee and a snack, hardly an earth-shattering moment in anyone's life.

'I'm not kidding. Put two Brits together and they'll spend most of their time discussing the vagaries of the weather. You'll never be at a loss for something to say if you stick to the weather as a topic.'

She burst out laughing. 'If I'd said that you would claim I was being racist!'

'Probably. But the one thing we British are good at is not taking ourselves too seriously. Right, two large cups of coffee coming up. And how about some bacon sandwiches to go with them?'

'No way! Think of all that cholesterol.' She shook her head so vigorously that a wisp of dark red hair broke free from its restraining pins.

Nick's hands clenched because he wasn't sure that he would be able to resist smoothing it back into place if he didn't get a grip on himself. How would she feel about that? he wondered, then cut short the answer because he didn't want to hear it. Even allowing himself to *imagine* that Leanne might not be averse to him touching her hair—or other parts of her beautiful body—was too big a test of his self-control.

'All right, then, no bacon. The sausage is pretty good, though, especially if you add lots of brown sauce... That's a thought. Do you Aussies appreciate the finer points of brown sauce? If not, your taste buds are in for a treat.'

He breathed a sigh of relief when she laughed. All things considered, he hadn't handled things too badly, he decided as they made their way to the nearest café. He'd kept his cool and hadn't made a complete idiot of himself. Great! Now all he had to do was keep it up for the next three months while Leanne worked at the clinic and he was home and dry.

Is that all? a small voice whispered. A mere twelve weeks of pretending that Leanne doesn't have the power to turn your life inside out? You have nothing to worry about, then, do you?

Nick swallowed a groan. Who was he kidding? Nothing about this situation was going to be easy. All he could do was pray that he had the strength of mind to stick to what he knew was right. No matter how much he liked Leanne, nothing could ever come of it.

'Just coffee and one of those rolls, please.'

Leanne pointed to a tray of sugary rolls at the back of the counter, nodding when the assistant asked if she wanted jam with it. 'Please.'

She took the plate and followed Nick to the checkout. Even at this early hour of the day, the café was crowded, but she spotted a couple getting up from a table in the corner and pointed towards it. 'I'll snag that table for us. OK?'

'Fine.' Nick gave her a quick smile then hunted some money out of his pocket to pay the cashier.

Leanne made her way to the table, edging aside the debris left by the previous diners so that she could put her tray down. She unloaded her cup and plate then piled the dirty dishes onto the tray and handed them to the young man who had arrived to clear up. By the time Nick arrived, the table had been wiped clean and she had managed to find paper napkins and silverware.

'How very organised you are, Miss Russell. I usually end up bobbing up and down, fetching all the things I've forgotten.' He unloaded his tray then grinned when he spotted the small packets of brown sauce propped against the salt cellar.

'You get extra points for those!' he said, laughing at her. 'Were you a Guide, by any chance? You seem to be very well prepared.'

'It comes from waiting on tables at my parents' restaurant, although brown sauce isn't something my dad normally offers his clientele,' she explained with a grin.

Nick's brows rose. 'Clientele, eh? I take it that your dad doesn't run a greasy-spoon café, then?'

'You take it right.' She ripped open a packet of sugar and poured it onto the frothy white bubbles floating on the surface of her cup of cappuccino. 'Dad caters for the top end of the market. The restaurant overlooks Sydney harbour and the people who go there expect—and get—the very best cuisine.'

'Sounds a great spot to dine,' he observed, cutting his sandwich in half. 'I spent six months in Sydney a few years back and fell in love with the place. The waterfront is stunning.'

'Melanie told me that you've travelled extensively,' she said, breaking off a piece of roll and liberally spreading it with strawberry conserve.

'I have.' He ate some of his bacon sandwich then wiped his mouth on a paper napkin before continuing. 'India, Africa, Australia and New Zealand, plus all kinds of places in between too numerous to mention.'

'Really? I'd never been out of Australia before I came to England,' she said. 'Did you always want to travel from way back when you were young?'

'Not at all.' He picked up his sandwich again and stared at it as though lost in thought.

'So what made you change your mind?' she prompted, because it seemed strangely important that she find out what his reasons had been.

'Oh, this and that, you know how it goes.' He bit into the bread and Leanne couldn't fail to see the sudden reserve in his eyes as he chewed it. 'So what made you decide to come to England, then?'

'It was a spur-of-the-moment decision,' she admitted, wondering what he was avoiding telling her. Maybe Nick's reasons for travelling the globe had nothing to do with her, but she couldn't help wishing that he'd told her more.

'Because you suddenly decided to come here with someone else?'

'Someone else?' She looked at him blankly, wondering what had caused that grating note in his voice.

'Uh-huh.' He leant towards her and she was surprised to see the urgency in his eyes. 'Are you here with your boyfriend, Leanne?'

'Boyfriend?' she repeated, then laughed out loud. 'Definitely not! Michael made it very clear that he thought I was crazy to come here.'

'I see.' He sat back in his seat and she was shocked when she saw how his hands were trembling when he picked up his cup.

What was wrong with him? she wondered giddily. Why did he look so *relieved* to learn that she was in London on her own?

The question spun through her mind and the answer followed it so fast that she had no time to shut it out. She bit her lip as a tremor ran through her. Nick was relieved because he hated the thought of her being here with another man.

It was an effort to control how elated that idea made her feel so it was a moment before she realised that he had asked her another question.

'I'm sorry. What did you say?' she asked, praying that he couldn't read her mind. The situation seemed to be spiralling out of control yet there was nothing she could do about it. She could no more stop herself feeling pleased about his reaction than she could have stopped herself breathing.

'I asked why you'd come to England if it wasn't to be with someone. You told me the other day that you weren't here to go sightseeing.'

'That's true. I'm not.' Leanne shrugged, not sure that she wanted to discuss the circumstances which had prompted her trip to England. She was still trying to come to terms with the discovery that she had been adopted and wasn't sure that she would be able to control her emotions if she had to explain it to Nick.

'Sorry.' He reached across the table and squeezed her hand. 'I didn't mean to pry. I just needed to know...' He stopped and she saw the strangest expression cross his face.

It prompted her to ask a question she knew deep down shouldn't be asked.

'Why, Nick?' she asked gently, her heart stalling because it felt as though something momentous was about to happen. 'Why did you *need* to know?'

'Because I want to know everything about you, Leanne. Your likes and dislikes, what makes you angry and sad. What gives you pleasure and causes you pain.'

His fingers tightened around hers but she knew that he wasn't aware that he was hurting her. 'I know it doesn't make sense, but I *need* to get to know you better even though we can never have a future together.'

Nick took a deep breath but his heart was hammering so hard that it felt as though it was going to shoot right out of his chest. Leanne was staring at him and he could see the shock in her eyes.

No damned wonder, he thought savagely, quickly withdrawing his hand. She probably thought he was a lunatic for coming out with a statement like that!

'Why can't we have a future, Nick?'

It was the last thing he had expected her to ask and it threw him into total confusion. He picked up his coffee-cup again then immediately put it down. Maybe he would regret this later, but he had left himself no choice other than to be honest with her.

'Because I'm not looking for commitment and never shall be,' he said bluntly, hating to see how she winced. His fingers curled around the cup because there was no way that he could risk holding her hand again when his emotions were so finely balanced.

'Never is a long time. You might change your mind.'

'I won't. I can't.'

'Can't? What do you mean by that?' Her eyes were luminous with unshed tears and it hurt to know that he was the cause of them. Of its own volition his hand reached out again and covered hers.

'Because I made a decision many years ago never to get

involved in a long-term relationship, and I can't go back on it,' he explained, knowing that he was glossing over the truth. If she pressed him, would he tell her the whole story? he wondered suddenly.

A few women had asked him to explain why he lived his life the way he did, but he'd always avoided giving them a direct answer. Yet if Leanne asked him, he knew that he would have to tell her, even though it was something he would prefer not to do. He didn't want her to think that he was looking for sympathy, neither did he want her to persuade him that he had made the wrong decision.

'And you had your reasons for making that decision, I don't doubt.' She smiled at him and her eyes were full of compassion. 'Maybe one day you will feel able to tell me, but I won't press you, Nick. I just think it's a shame that you're denying yourself so much.'

'I enjoy my life,' he said shortly, somewhat stung by the remark as well as by the thought that he might have made a mistake. He knew that it was the only choice he could have made in the circumstances. 'I do a job I love and I get to see far more of the world than most people could dream of seeing. I'm certainly not unhappy.'

'Of course not, and I wasn't implying that you were.'

Leanne withdrew her hand abruptly and he had to stop himself from reaching for it again as she picked up her cup and sipped a little of the coffee. She placed the cup carefully back on the table then looked him squarely in the eyes.

'I know there's something between us, Nick. I felt it yesterday when we met and I can feel it now. Maybe it's good old-fashioned sexual attraction and maybe it's something more, but I don't think either of us is in a position to dig too deeply into how we feel at the moment. You asked me why I came to England and maybe it would be best if I told you.'

'You don't have to tell me anything you don't want to,' he said quickly, his head reeling from her honesty. Was it purely desire they felt for one another? Or was it more than that, as she'd just hinted?

His mind shied away from what that 'more' could be because it was ridiculous to think such a thing. Leanne was speaking again and he made himself focus on what she was saying, feeling a spasm shoot through him when he heard the pain in her voice.

'My mother died two months ago. It wasn't a complete shock because she had been ill for some time. She'd had rheumatic fever as a child and had always had heart problems.

'It hit Dad very hard, though, so after the funeral I offered to sort out her belongings to make it a bit easier for him. It was while I was going through some old papers that I discovered I had been adopted as a baby. I'd had no idea until then.'

Nick frowned, trying to imagine how she must have felt. 'It must have been a shock for you.'

'It was. All of a sudden I didn't know who I was any more. It felt as though I'd been living a lie all my life because I wasn't the person I'd believed myself to be.'

'That's crazy!' he exclaimed. 'You're the same person you've always been, Leanne. Just because your mother and father aren't your natural parents, it doesn't change that.'

'Maybe not.' She gave him a small smile that made his heart ache because it was obvious how much the discovery had upset her. 'Anyway, I decided that I had to find out about my birth mother. Once Dad realised how important it was to me, he did all he could to help. He has never said so, but I got the impression that it was Mum who was so opposed to me being told the truth rather than Dad.'

'Maybe she was afraid that it might have changed how you felt about them as parents,' he suggested gently.

'I expect you're right. But I don't blame them for not telling me the truth because I know they did what they thought was best for me,' she said firmly. 'They were—are—the most wonderful parents anyone could have and I feel so lucky that they were the people who adopted me. It's just that I would like to find out something about my background and why I was given up for adoption.'

'Understandable, of course. So how far have you got? Have you managed to trace your birth mother?'

'Not yet. I was adopted privately, you see, through a church charity. Mum and Dad were still living in London at the time—they moved to Sydney when I was a year old.' She carried on when Nick nodded. 'Anyway, Dad tried to get in touch with the people who used to run the adoption scheme, but it turned out that it's no longer in existence.'

'That must have made things rather difficult,' he said.

'It has. Apparently, the charity's records have been lodged with the Family Records Centre here in London, so I emailed them before I left Sydney, asking if I would be able to view my file when I arrived. They wrote back to say that it would be several weeks before my birth records were available because of the volume of applications they have to deal with.'

'That leaves you rather in a state of limbo at the moment, doesn't it? Or do you have another line of enquiry to follow?'

'Fortunately, Dad had kept a copy of my original birth certificate. It gives my mother's name as Mary Calhoun, along with an address in Camden where she was living at the time I was born. I decided not to delay my trip but to use the information I had to try and find her.' She shrugged. 'That's it, basically.'

'Except that a situation like this is never simple.'

'No, you're right. It's been stressful for a number of reasons. Dad was terribly upset at first when I told him what I was planning on doing. He felt that he and Mum must have done something wrong if I felt that I needed to find this other woman. It took me a while to convince him that it had nothing whatsoever to do with that. And as for Michael, my boyfriend...well, he was *extremely* put out about having his plans disrupted because I was coming to England.'

'Are you sure about that?' he queried. Admittedly, it had caused him a pang to hear her mention the other man's name, but it was Leanne's feelings he was more concerned about. 'Surely he was more worried about you coming all this way on your own than anything else?'

'Nice thought, but it isn't true. Michael was annoyed because it would mean him having to delay announcing our engagement. He had decided to make the announcement at the staff Christmas party and that was it. He wouldn't listen when I tried to explain how important this trip was to me.'

She shrugged. 'Still, maybe it was a good thing that I found out what he was like sooner rather than later. It's easier to end an engagement than a marriage.'

'Maybe you'll change your mind once you return home,' he suggested, hoping that his elation didn't show. It didn't make him feel good to know that he was pleased because Leanne had broken up with her boyfriend, but he couldn't help it.

'I doubt it. To be honest, I'd been having doubts before all this happened. It was obvious that Michael and I held different views on a lot of things.'

'Such as?' he prompted, knowing the he shouldn't really probe yet unable to stop himself.

'Like having a family, for instance. I would love to have children and I don't want to leave it until I'm too old to enjoy them. Michael, however, made no bones about the fact that he doesn't want a family for ages. I think he's worried that it might mean him having to give up all his expensive holidays and cars, things like that.'

'Difficult,' Nick said, praying that she couldn't tell how much it had hurt him to hear that. Knowing that Leanne longed to have children was intensely painful because it brought it home to him how wrong it would be for them to get involved. He would never have children, not after what he'd discovered when Matt had been taken ill. It was an effort to hide his feelings when she continued.

'Anyway, so here I am in London, searching for the woman who gave me away, and I meet you.'

'And?' he asked, feeling his heart jerk nervously.

'*And* I'm not sure what we do about it.' She gave him a long, hard look. 'Where do we go from here, Nick? You aren't interested in a long-term relationship and I *know* it's the completely wrong time for me to get involved when my life is up in the air. So how do we solve this little problem?'

He took a deep breath because he knew this was probably the most important moment of his entire life. Whatever decision he made now would affect his whole future.

His mind spasmed with pain because the future was something he'd always refused to think about. It was the here and now that mattered, what happened today, not tomorrow. But would Leanne see things the way he did?

'How about we agree to be friends for starters?' he suggested, hoping that she couldn't hear the ache in his voice. 'Then we can wait and see what happens. So long as we both understand the limits, there shouldn't be a problem.'

'No, there shouldn't,' she agreed quietly. She stared at the table for a moment then suddenly picked up her cup and held it aloft. 'Here's to friendship, then. Let the rest take care of itself. OK?'

'OK.' He clinked his cup against hers and smiled, but his heart felt like lead all of a sudden. Friendship would never be enough with this woman. He wanted more than that, a whole lot more, but he couldn't have it. He had to be content with what they had for however long it lasted, although deep down he knew that eternity wouldn't be long enough.

He wanted Leanne in his life for ever, but it wasn't going to happen.

'It's just a couple of small scratches on your arm. They won't really hurt, Peter. And just think what fun you'll have when you go on your holiday after Christmas.'

Leanne smiled at the little boy but it was obvious that he wasn't convinced by her reassurances. Peter Goode had been brought into the clinic by his parents' housekeeper to have vaccinations against typhoid and hepatitis A. The family was flying to Mexico in the New Year and had been advised that they needed protection against both these diseases.

Peter had made such a fuss each time his mother had tried to take him to their own GP that she'd asked the housekeeper to bring him to the clinic instead. It had been hoped that the change of venue—allied to a visit to the Natural History Museum—might help. It didn't seem to be working, unfortunately.

'Don't want them!' the nine year-old screamed. 'No, no no!'

'Peter, stop that! You know Mummy will be cross if we go home and tell her that you wouldn't have the injections again.' Angela Wainwright, the family's housekeeper, looked despairingly at Leanne. 'I just don't know what to do. We've tried everything from bribery to threats. I really and truly thought the visit to the museum would help, but it's hopeless.'

'It's often difficult with children,' she said consolingly, thinking fast. She needed to find a way to distract the child so that he was thinking about something else rather than what was about to happen.

If only she could apply that same reasoning to herself, she thought wryly as she excused herself and hurried to the staffroom. But no matter how many distractions there had been that morning, she couldn't stop thinking about the conversation she'd had with Nick. They had agreed to be friends, but how long would they be content with that situation when it was obvious they both wanted more?

Melanie was in the staffroom with Sergio Alesi, a doctor from Milan. They looked up when Leanne went in and Melanie gave her a conspiratorial grin.

'The joys of dealing with kids, eh? I take it that you weren't actually trying to kill the little dear?'

'No. Just trying to give him a couple of injections, believe it or not,' she explained as she went to her locker and found the apple she had brought for her morning break. She hadn't eaten it because she'd been full from that snack she'd had with Nick. She sighed when her mind immediately whizzed back again to what had happened.

'So what do you intend to do with that?' Sergio asked when he saw what she had in her hand. 'Lace it with some kind of tranquilliser and feed it to him so that you can give him the jabs while he's asleep?'

'Nice idea, but I think his parents might object,' she declared, grinning at him.

Sergio was very good-looking with jet black hair and the most soulful brown eyes. She suspected that Melanie was more than a little smitten with the handsome young Italian and could understand why although he didn't have the same effect on her. Sergio couldn't hold a candle to Nick, in her opinion.

She glanced round when the door opened, feeling a wash of colour run up her face when she saw Nick. She hurriedly turned back to the others and finished explaining her plan to them, terrified that Nick might guess what had been going through her mind. The only way they would deal with this attraction they felt for each other was by keeping things low-key.

'Don't make yourself late, Leanne.' He smiled as he opened the door for her, but she couldn't help noticing how strained he looked. 'You're due to finish soon, aren't you?'

'A few extra minutes won't make any difference,' she assured him.

She frowned as she left the staffroom, wondering why he had appeared so tense. Because he regretted what he'd said that morning and wished he hadn't been so open about his feelings?

It was the only explanation she could come up with, but it was upsetting to know that he regretted what had happened. Surely Nick understood that it was better to be honest in a situation like this?

There was no time to resolve the problem, unfortunately,

not when she had a patient waiting. Peter looked warily at her when she went back into the treatment room and closed the door.

'I'm not having any needles stuck into me,' he declared fiercely.

'Fine. It's up to you, of course. I'm not going to force you, neither is Mrs Wainwright.' She shook her head when the housekeeper went to speak and the woman obligingly fell silent.

Moving to the desk, Leanne placed the apple on the blotter then took an empty syringe from the box. 'I think I'll just have a little practice by injecting this apple. I have some more people who need injections this afternoon.'

She slid the needle into the skin of the fruit and pretended to inject it, watching Peter out of the corner of her eyes. He was obviously intrigued by what she was doing and moved closer so that he could watch her. Leanne did it a couple more times then glanced at him.

'Want to have a go?'

'Can I?' He took the syringe from her and listened carefully while she explained how to slip the point of the needle very gently into the skin of the apple so as not to bruise it. He tried it himself, smiling with delight when he discovered how easy it was.

'That's all that will happen if I give you the injections,' she told him gently. 'I just slip the needle into your skin and that's it.'

'And it really doesn't hurt?' he said cautiously.

'Just a little, about the same as if you prick yourself with a pin. Shall we give it a go and see how we get on?'

'I s'ppose so.' He was still very wary, but he stood still while she swabbed his arm with alcohol. He barely flinched when she administered the first injection and he looked at her in surprise.

'I hardly felt that!'

'Good. Shall we do the other one now or do you want to

leave it until another day? It's up to you, Peter. You can always come back again to see me.'

'Do it now,' he said firmly.

Leanne administered the second vaccination then ruffled his hair. 'That's it. All done. You can go to the Natural History Museum now and see the dinosaurs.'

'They're my favourite,' he told her, smiling happily now that the ordeal was over. 'I've got lots and *lots* of model dinosaurs at home and Angela said that she would buy me another one if I was good today. I have been good, haven't I?' he asked, shooting an uncertain glance at the housekeeper.

'Very good and very brave, too.' Angela gave him a hug then smiled at Leanne. 'Bless you. You really put him at his ease and I appreciate that.'

'It was my pleasure. And who knows? Peter might decide to become a doctor one day and give people injections. He's obviously very good at it.'

'I want to be a scientist and grow dinosaurs like in that film,' he told her importantly.

Leanne frowned. 'From what I can remember, the scientists needed to inject the dinosaur DNA into the eggs to create baby dinosaurs, so you're halfway there.'

'Wicked!' Peter declared, beaming. 'I can't wait to tell Mum and Dad when they get home from work!'

He was still smiling when he left. Leanne tidied up, thinking how it was often the strangest things that captured a child's imagination. Her own childhood had been extremely happy because her parents had given her the space to develop her own interests and had supported everything she'd done.

She couldn't have had two more wonderful people to raise her, in fact, but she still needed to find out about her background, join up all the dots so that she could see the whole picture. After that, she could get on with her life.

She finished clearing up then realised it was time she left. She went to the staffroom to fetch her coat, feeling her heart surge when she found Nick still in there. He looked up and smiled, but she could see the shadows in his eyes and it bothered her to see them.

'I'm taking an early lunch because we're short-staffed this afternoon,' he explained. 'Robert has phoned in sick with a cold.'

'Do you want me to stay?' she offered, but he shook his head.

'No, it's fine. I know you've got things to do. What have you got planned for this afternoon?'

'Checking out the local parish church where my mother lived. They might have records that will help me trace her if she stayed in the area and eventually got married there,' she said shortly, because she couldn't help feeling a little put out by his instant refusal of her offer to help.

'They might.' He suddenly sighed. 'I can tell you're annoyed, Leanne. It isn't that I don't appreciate you offering to stay.'

'But? There was a definite *but* in there, Nick.'

'Yes, there was. *But* I think it would be best for both of us if we had a breathing space. I'm finding it extremely difficult to keep my mind on my work after that talk we had this morning.'

'You, too?' she exclaimed, then blushed when she realised how revealing that had been.

'Uh-huh.' He laughed, his eyes sparkling with amusement. 'Seems as though we're both in the same boat, doesn't it?'

He smiled broadly when she nodded. 'I don't know if that's a good or a bad thing, but I do know that we need to do something about it. How about joining me for a drink tonight while we work out a plan of campaign?'

'Do you think that's wise?' she queried. They had agreed to be friends, but could they stick to that if they saw each other outside working hours?

'Probably not. But I'd hate to end up regretting not spending some time with you while you're in England, Leanne.'

'Me, too,' she agreed softly and knew it was true. Maybe they would only have a few weeks together, but she didn't want to look back on this period in her life in years to come and wish that she had done things differently. Whatever happened, she would meet it head on. She just had to remember the one basic rule—that neither of them was looking for commitment.

It was only when she was on her way home, having arranged to meet Nick at a local wine bar that evening, that the old saying about rules being made to be broken came flooding back. But it was too late to change her mind by that point.

Far too late.

CHAPTER FOUR

IT WAS a busy day so that by the time Nick locked up the clinic at eight-thirty that evening, he was feeling totally drained. Robert's absence had meant that he and Sergio had needed to pull out all the stops to keep up with the number of patients who had asked to see a GP.

The situation had eased slightly at five o'clock when two more doctors had come on duty. However, they were both new to the clinic and he had felt it was essential to oversee their work. Fortunately HealthFirst's policy of only employing staff with the highest qualifications meant that both had proved themselves to be more than capable of doing the job, but it had added to his workload. He was flagging when he reached the wine bar where he had arranged to meet Leanne, and it didn't help to discover that the place was packed.

He propped himself up against the bar and ordered a glass of red wine. The man next to him was smoking so he turned to face the other way to avoid having smoke blown into his eyes. Consequently, he didn't see Leanne arriving and jumped when he heard her voice behind him.

'Hi, there!'

He turned to face her, feeling hot little shivers of awareness dancing along his nerves. It was the first time he had seen her casually dressed and he couldn't help staring because she looked so lovely.

She was wearing khaki jeans with a cream-coloured fleece top. The jeans emphasised the length of her shapely legs whilst the cream colour was the perfect foil for her tanned skin. Her hair was loose that night, instead of being drawn back off her face, the dark red strands glittering as they caught the light. Without stopping to think what he was doing, he reached out and ran one silky strand through his fingers.

'You have the most beautiful hair,' he said, his voice sounding unnaturally thick and heavy as it emerged from his throat.

'Thank you.'

She gave a rueful laugh, but he could see from the way her eyes had darkened how the compliment had affected her. 'I hated having red hair when I was kid. I was always the one the neighbours picked out if me and my friends got into trouble. I can't count the number of times some irate soul knocked on our front door, baying for my blood!'

Nick burst out laughing. 'You really expect me to believe that you were some kind of junior tearaway?'

'Too right.' She grinned as she squeezed into the gap beside him. 'I was a real tomboy. I climbed trees, stole apples from the neighbours' gardens, knocked on doors then hid...you name it and I did it. It's a wonder I reached adulthood, believe me!'

'It's difficult, I promise you.' Nick signalled to the barman then glanced at her. 'What do you fancy to drink?'

'Something not laced with cigarette smoke,' she replied tartly, giving the man beside them a speaking look.

'Now, that might be rather difficult to arrange. Unfortunately, there aren't too many bars in London which have adopted a no-smoking policy,' he explained ruefully.

'The sooner they do so, the better for all concerned,' she replied, wafting a hand in front of her face to drive away the smoke.

It was obvious the smoke was causing her some discomfort so Nick quickly considered his options. They could find another bar but there was no guarantee that it would be any healthier than this one was. Of course, they could always go back to his flat and have a drink. He had a couple of bottles of wine in the fridge.

'How about if we went to my flat and had a drink?' he suggested before he could think better of it. Alarm bells were ringing inside his head and a small voice was shrieking in his ear, *Bad idea!* But he chose to ignore them. After all, they were two sane and sensible adults, well versed in the ways of the world. If they couldn't handle being alone together, who could?

'I'm not sure it would be wise,' she said, looking at him with steady grey eyes.

'Tempting fate?' he suggested, striving for levity.

'Something like that.' She treated him to a smile then coughed when another cloud of smoke drifted in their direction. 'Mind you, the alternative of risking our health by staying here is a lot less appealing.'

'We could always go somewhere else. There's a couple more wine bars along the road.'

'And will they be as smoky as this one?' She sighed when he shrugged. 'I'll take that as a yes. Seems that we don't have much choice. It's your flat or abandon our plans for the evening.'

'We could do that if you prefer,' he said, hoping that she couldn't tell how disappointed he felt. It hit him then how much he had been looking forward to seeing her that night, but maybe it *would* be wiser to take the sensible option.

'I don't.'

Nick's eyes snapped to her face when he heard the certainty in her voice and he felt his heart start to bounce up and down like a child on a pogo-stick.

'So it's back to my flat, then?' he said, trying his best to calm things down. If his heart kept on like that, there was a very real danger that he wouldn't make it as far as his flat. He would probably keel over right here at her feet!

'Why not? After all, we both understand the rules, don't we, Nick? So there's no problem.'

Once again he was struck by Leanne's apparent confidence and once again wished that he shared it. However, as he put his glass back on the counter, he knew that he had never felt less sure of anything in his life.

Could he behave with the utmost propriety towards

Leanne when every instinct was clamouring for him to do the opposite? Could he stick to the promise they had made that morning to remain friends and not want more? Could he focus solely on the present and not start thinking about the future?

He sighed as he followed her to the door. What a lot of *coulds* and what a dearth of *woulds*. Nothing was guaranteed in this situation. Emotions couldn't be ring-fenced with warranties giving one hundred per cent protection. He had to take each minute as it came and not worry about what might happen tomorrow or the day after.

They were the rules by which he'd lived since Matt had died, but all of a sudden he wasn't sure that he would be able to stick to them. How he felt about Leanne went way beyond the scope of any rule book.

Leanne knew in her heart that she might come to regret this decision. As she walked along the street her heart was pounding with nerves. Going back to Nick's flat was tempting fate when they were both so vulnerable.

'It's just down here.'

He touched her lightly on the shoulder to point her in the right direction when they reached the end of the road, and she bit her lip. Even through the thickness of two sweaters and an arctic fleece she could feel the heat of his hand. Blood cells were already queuing up in her veins to absorb some of that heat and rush it around her body, and she couldn't begin to imagine the effect that would have.

Deliberately, she moved so that his hand fell away then immediately felt bereft when she was denied the contact. It was an effort to behave as though nothing was wrong when it felt as though she had suffered some massive loss.

'I've not been this way before. My explorations have been confined to the area around St Stephen's station and the part of Camden Town where my mother lived.'

'So you've not done any sightseeing?' he queried in surprise.

'None. Maybe I'll get around to it before I return home, but at the moment my main concern is finding out about my mother,' she explained.

'I can understand that, but it would be a shame to come all this way and not see what London has to offer.'

He paused to smile at her, his teeth gleaming whitely in the gloom. Several of the streetlights didn't appear to be working and the road was rather dark. Leanne could barely make out the winter-thin outlines of the trees in the small park at the centre of the square. There was no one about and it gave her an odd, shivery feeling inside to know that she and Nick were alone in the darkness.

'I suppose it would,' she conceded, carrying on walking because she wasn't sure how to deal with that thought or the one that followed it. When she went back to his flat, they really would be alone—and how would she feel then?

It was impossible to answer that question and the fact that she had such difficulty doing so simply added to her tension. They carried on in silence until Nick stopped outside one of the houses that bordered the square.

'This is it. Are you ready for the heady experience of seeing my home-sweet-home for the first time?'

His voice grated even though he'd adopted a deliberately joking tone. Leanne's tension increased that little bit more. Nick was just as concerned about whether this was the right thing to do, so how could she be sure that they weren't making a mistake?

'You can still change your mind, Leanne. You don't have to do anything you don't feel happy about.'

She heard the understanding in his voice as well as the concern and all of a sudden her uncertainties melted away. Nick wouldn't do anything she didn't want him to do. She had complete trust in him. Maybe they needed to face up to how they felt instead of trying to avoid the issue because their feelings certainly weren't going to go away.

'I know that, but I'd really like to see your flat, Nick.' She smiled at him, loving the way his eyes immediately filled with warmth. 'I'd also like that glass of wine you promised me. Maybe it will help to thaw me out. It's *freezing* out here!'

'This isn't cold,' he retorted, hunting the key out of his pocket. 'Cold is when the water in the Serpentine freezes and your breath makes those puffy little clouds when you speak. Remember doing that when you were a child, breathing out as hard as you could so you could see your breath freezing?'

'Sorry, but you forget I come from a place where the weather is more civilised,' she shot back with a grin.

'It might be more civilised, but you don't know what you've been missing.'

He opened the door and led the way into the house, pausing to switch on the hall lights. 'You had a deprived childhood, Leanne Russell. Matt and I used to spend hours each winter trying to see who could puff out the biggest cloud.'

'You must miss him,' she said softly.

'I do.' He took a deep breath and she felt her heart ache when she saw the pain in his eyes. 'I still find it hard to believe that he's gone even after all these years.'

'Oh, Nick, I wish there was something I could say to help.'

It seemed the most natural thing in the world to follow through with that thought. She didn't even pause as she reached up and kissed him on the cheek. It was meant purely as a token of comfort, yet it had a galvanising effect.

Leanne's heart stalled when she felt the roughness of his skin beneath her lips. He must have shaved before he had left for work that morning and his beard was coming through again. She could feel the tiny barbs prickling her skin, feel how her lips snagged against them when she moved her mouth a fraction of an inch...

'Don't do that, Leanne!'

The strain in his voice made her realise what she was doing and she quickly stepped back. Her face felt as though it was on fire when she saw the awareness in his eyes, the need. Her body was throbbing, shivers of sensation pulsing through her as reaction set in, and yet all she'd done had been to kiss him on the cheek.

'I'm sorry,' she said tightly, turning blindly towards the stairs.

'It doesn't matter. This way.' He automatically put out his hand to stop her then obviously thought better of touching her. He nodded instead towards a door at the end of the hall. 'My flat's on the ground floor. It means that I don't have to stagger up dozens of stairs when I get home from work.'

'A definite advantage,' she agreed, struggling to respond in the same light vein. She owed it to him not to make an issue of what had happened, but it wasn't easy to contain the emotions welling inside her.

How was it possible to feel such desire for this man? she wondered as she followed him down the hall. Maybe she should explain it away as simple sexual attraction, but it didn't seem enough to class it as that. What she felt for Nick Slater went deeper than that and it scared her to admit it. It was an effort to behave naturally when he turned to her after unlocking his front door.

'Ladies first.'

'Thank you.'

Leanne stepped into the tiny entrance hall, easing past the bicycle that was propped against the wall by the door. There wasn't much room to pass and she grimaced when the pocket of her fleece jacket snagged on the handlebars. She stopped to disentangle herself then gasped when the bike toppled towards her.

'Careful!' Nick leant over and grabbed it. He propped it back up against the wall then turned to her in concern. 'Are you all right? It didn't hurt you?'

'I'm fine.'

Leanne took a quick breath but her heart was racing, and not because of the fright she'd had. They were standing so close now that she could feel the warmth of Nick's body and smell the clean scent of his skin. All of a sudden her senses seemed to be working overtime so that it felt as though she had never been so aware of anyone before.

When he reached out and touched her, just lightly, on the arm she jumped and felt him flinch as well. It was though their nerve endings were suddenly able to transmit signals to each other, sending messages from her body to his. The idea enthralled her.

Could he feel how much she wanted him? Because she could tell how much he wanted her.

His hands were hard and strong when he suddenly pulled her to him yet once he had her in his arms he held her with such tenderness that it brought a lump to her throat. Nick would use his strength to protect and cherish, never to overwhelm or force. He framed her face between his hands and his eyes were full of wonderment when he looked at her.

'I don't know what's happening any more. Why do I feel like this, Leanne? How can I want you so much? Can you explain it? Because I can't.'

'Maybe there isn't an explanation,' she said softly, tears welling in her eyes because of the intensity of what they were feeling. 'And maybe it's wrong for us to try to work it out.'

'You mean that we should just go with the flow,' he said, smiling at her, and the fact that he could joke at a time like that was a measure of the man he was. Nick didn't try to set himself on a pedestal. He didn't pretend to be what he wasn't. He was open and honest about himself and his feelings.

It was another little nugget to add to the store of things she knew about him, and she savoured it greedily as she smiled at him. 'I suppose it all depends where the flow is taking us.'

'I'm not sure about that either, I'm afraid. What I can tell you is that if I don't kiss you soon I'll probably pass out. I'm a man *in extremis*, Leanne. Have pity!'

Laughter bubbled from her throat, escaped her lips then was trapped by his mouth. Leanne felt a deep shudder of relief run through her as she felt his lips settling on hers, and it was only then that she realised how much she'd needed this to happen. The thought melted away any last reservations she'd had.

She twined her arms around his neck while she deepened the kiss, feeling his lips immediately part when she teased them with her tongue. Their tongues met, danced together then withdrew, and all the time their passion was building, growing hotter and more demanding.

When Nick reluctantly pulled back they were both breathing heavily, both trembling, both aware that they had reached a point when they had to make a decision about what happened next. Maybe they also knew what it would be, but there were rules to adhere to first, courtesies to observe in the ritual leading up to love-making. Oddly enough, they added an extra edge to the tension in the air.

'What happens now?' he asked quietly, his eyes holding hers in a look she couldn't and wouldn't break.

'What do you want to happen?' she countered, playing the game which was both a torment and a delight. The fact that she had never played this game with any man before—not even Michael—didn't surprise her. This situation was different to any she had encountered. *Nick* was different. Special. It was no wonder that it felt like the very first time.

'I want to take you to my bed and make love to you until we're both dizzy,' he grated. 'I want to hold you in my arms and fall asleep then wake up still holding you in the morning and make love to you all over again. Does that shock you, Leanne? Does it scare you? Because it scares the hell out of me!'

'Because you hadn't bargained on this happening? Or because you had convinced yourself that you wouldn't let it happen?'

Leanne laughed when she saw from his rueful expression that both were true. 'Me, too, Nick. I'm just as shocked as you are. Maybe I'm just as scared because I don't know how this is going to work out. I don't make a habit of jumping into bed with a man I've known for less than forty-eight hours, I assure you.'

'Neither do I make a habit of jumping into bed with a woman I've only known for that length of time. But how long we've known each other is irrelevant, Leanne,' he declared with a touching trace of arrogance. 'You can know someone for years and yet *not* know them…'

'And you can know someone for less than two days and feel as though you've found your soul-mate,' she put in quietly, unable to lie. She heard him take a quick breath and knew what he was going to say.

'No.' She put her fingers against his lips, stemming the words, not needing to hear them. 'What we agreed still stands, Nick. Neither of us wants commitment at the moment.'

'Then what do we want?' He moved her hand away from his mouth and held it tightly. 'You tell me, Leanne, because I'm not sure black is black any longer!'

She shook her head, feeling sparks flashing through her body and setting alight the passion that was simmering inside her. 'I don't need to tell you, Nick, because you know what the answer is.'

She had barely finished speaking when he lifted her into his arms. His mouth found hers and she gasped when she felt the rawness of his desire. Nick was kissing her as though he was starving for the taste of her, and maybe he was. It felt as though she had been starving for him all her life.

He carried her into the tiny bedroom and laid her down on the narrow, single bed with its worn candlewick spread as though he was laying her on a silken couch fit for a princess. There was only the light from the hall flowing into the room so his face was partly in shadow when he bent over her, but she could see enough to know that he was telling her the truth.

'I swear on my life that I shall never do anything to hurt you, Leanne. I…I care too much about you.'

Her heart ached because she knew what he had wanted to

say and what he couldn't bring himself to utter. Maybe he was right, too, because it really was too soon to be talking about love. Far better to stick to something simple like the way they were feeling.

She closed her eyes as he kissed her again, feeling the hot tide of passion lapping closer to the surface with each second that passed. His lips were hard and demanding then soft and tender, giving and taking. The contrasts were so sharp, so acute, that she could only react to them.

She kissed him back, returned his caresses, held and coaxed him, and never had she felt such a wealth of emotions before. When he drew the fleece over her head and followed it with the first of her jumpers she started trembling, and it just got worse when he removed the second sweater and she was lying before him in just her bra and a thin silk vest.

He threw his coat onto the floor, tossed his shirt after it then smiled at her. 'I'm not sure if it's more frustrating to have to get rid of all these layers or simply tantalising. What do you think?'

She let her palms slide over his chest, feeling the smoothness of his cotton T-shirt beneath her palms and the heat of his skin beneath that. 'The jury's still out on that one. You'll have to wait for the verdict, I'm afraid.'

Nick laughed deeply as he linked his fingers through hers and raised her hands above her head. 'Then I'd better start putting together a good case, hadn't I?'

His mouth nuzzled her nipple through the silky layers of her underwear and she gasped. 'You're obviously very persuasive. Maybe you should have gone in for law instead of medicine.'

'Maybe I should…'

The rest of the sentence was bitten off because it was obvious that he found it too distracting to talk. Leanne closed her eyes, feeling ripples of fire dancing along her veins as Nick kissed her breasts then removed her vest and bra and kissed them all over again.

Blindly she reached out and grasped the hem of his T-shirt, dragging it up his body and over his head between kisses. She couldn't resist looking at him and her heart went wild when she saw the powerful muscles under the tanned skin, the thick dark hair that arrowed down below his belt...

She closed her eyes again but she could still see his image imprinted on her retinas as passion rose and swelled inside her. Nerve endings were popping with static, her blood was flowing like liquid fire and her heart was racing, yet she was aware of every single thing that was happening in a way that she had never been before. Each touch of Nick's hands on her hot skin made her burn all the more, every brush of his lips over the most sensitive parts of her body made her tingle. She had never felt more alive than she did at that moment, making love with him.

'We need to be sensible about one thing, sweetheart.'

Leanne's eyes flew open when she felt him pulling away from her. 'Nick...?'

He bent and kissed her when he heard the panic in her voice. 'I'll only be a second. We don't want to complicate matters, do we?'

Leanne bit her lip when he went into the adjoining bathroom and reappeared with a foil-wrapped package containing a condom. She couldn't believe that she had given no thought to the consequences of their actions. She had been on the Pill when she and Michael had been engaged, but she had stopped taking it after they'd split up. There had been no point taking precautions against something that wasn't going to happen, she had reasoned. But that went to show how wrong she had been.

'Hey, it's OK.' Nick frowned when he saw her expression. 'It's easy to get carried away, Leanne.'

'You weren't,' she said stiffly, and that thought hurt more than a little. Even in the throes of passion Nick had thought about taking precautions. Why? Because he wasn't as deeply affected by what was happening as she was? She couldn't bear it if this was just a one-night stand to him!

'No, because I made myself remember what I had told you.' He gently turned her towards him and looked into her eyes. 'I promised you that I would never do anything to hurt you, and this is all part and parcel of it.'

There was no way that she could doubt that he was telling her the truth and the cold little knot that had twisted her insides suddenly melted. 'Thank you,' she whispered.

'You're welcome.'

He ran his finger across the freckles on her nose then kissed her lightly on the mouth, only the kiss somehow ended up being anything but light. Leanne gasped as passion flared between them again. It was impossible to think of anything except how wonderful it was to feel Nick's arms around her, to feel his powerful body joining with hers.

They made love with a depth and intensity that left them both shaken. When it was over neither of them really knew what to say. Nick took a deep breath then reached for the robe that was tossed over the end of the bed and got up.

'I'll open that wine. There should be plenty of hot water if you want a shower.' He belted the robe around him then bent to kiss her gently on the mouth. 'I shall never forget this night, Leanne. It was very special.'

'It was special for me, too,' she whispered.

She watched him leave the room then got out of bed and went into the bathroom. The water was hot, as he had promised, and she stood beneath it for a long time while she tried to make sense of what had happened.

She had never done anything like this in her life. The only man she had slept with had been Michael and then only after he'd asked her to marry him. Jumping into bed with a stranger was something she had abhorred even though several of her friends seemed to think nothing of it. Maybe she should feel guilty or ashamed but she felt neither of those things. She didn't regret making love with Nick and never would, no matter how it turned out.

She switched off the shower and her heart felt heavy all of a sudden because she knew how it would end. No commitment. No promises. No happily-ever-after. She had gone into this with her eyes wide open and she wouldn't make the mistake of seeing the situation for more than it was.

At the end of her stay in London she would go home to Sydney and Nick would go wherever it was he planned on going next. There certainly wasn't any future for them.

'I saw you and Leanne coming out of the wine bar last night. You're a dark horse, Nick Slater. I thought you told me you weren't interested in women at the moment?'

Nick frowned when he looked up and saw Dennis standing in the doorway to his office. He had come into work early that day simply because he hadn't been able to stand being in his flat any longer. The place had felt so empty since Leanne had left.

She had refused the glass of wine he'd poured for her, claiming that she needed to get home if she hoped to be fit for work the following day. He'd guessed that it had been an excuse. Leanne hadn't been able to stop herself last night. She had been as overwhelmed by the feelings they'd aroused in each other as he had been. If he'd been less cynical, he might have found himself wondering if love at first sight actually *did* exist.

'And I meant it,' he said tersely, struggling to rid himself of that idea. He wasn't interested in falling in love. It was the last thing he needed! 'Leanne and I went for a drink, that's all.'

'All? That I very much doubt.' Dennis winked at him. 'Come on, admit it, you fancy the lovely Leanne, don't you? I don't blame you because she's a real peach...'

'If you haven't any work to do, I have,' Nick snapped in an uncharacteristic show of bad temper. It irked him to hear the other man speaking about Leanne in such a fashion. He bit back a groan when he saw the speculation on Dennis's face.

'Touchy this morning, aren't we? Could it be that the lovely Leanne turned you down last night after all?' Dennis laughed good-naturedly. 'Never mind, if you didn't manage to get her into your bed last night, Nick, I'm sure there'll be other occasions...'

'Excuse me, but there's a patient waiting to see you, Dr Slater. Mr James Rogers. He has an appointment for a physical examination at eight-thirty, but he was wondering if you might be able to see him now.'

Nick froze when he recognised those cool tones. It was like a nightmare rerun of the day Leanne had arrived. His heart was already sinking towards his boots before he looked up, and the moment he saw the hurt in her eyes it rapidly finished its descent.

'Yes, of course. You can show him straight through,' he said, knowing that guilt must be written all over his face even though he wasn't at fault. It was Dennis who had been talking about getting Leanne into his bed, although he doubted if she would attribute the blame to the other man.

He shot to his feet when she turned to leave, uncaring what Dennis thought as he hurried after her. He simply couldn't let her leave, thinking the worst.

'Leanne, wait!' he pleaded, following her out to the corridor and catching hold of her arm.

'What for?' Her mouth curled into a smile, but the pain in her eyes told a very different story about how she was feeling. 'I don't think there's much to say, Nick. I only hope that you won't regale Dennis with all the gory details, but that's up to you, of course. It all depends on how keen you are to win that bet, I imagine.'

'This has got nothing whatsoever to do with any damned bet!' he exploded.

He glanced round, realising that they were standing in full view of anyone coming along the corridor. The supply cupboard was the closest spot where they could have some privacy, but Leanne wrenched her arm out of his grasp when he tried to lead her towards it.

'I am not going anywhere with you, Nick,' she said, carefully enunciating each word. 'The subject is closed. Now, you have a patient waiting so shall I show him through to your office?'

'Please.' It was an effort to force out the single word but he knew it was pointless trying to make her see sense right then. She was hurt and angry, as she had every right to be.

He went back to his office, relieved to find that Dennis had had the sense to leave. Frankly, he was at a loss to know what to do. He *had* to make Leanne understand that last night had had nothing to do with any stupid bet...

Did he *really* need to do that? a small voice inside him cut in. Bearing in mind that crazy idea he'd had about it being love at first sight, might it not be better to let her continue thinking the worst of him? The plain truth was that he and Leanne could never have a future together, so maybe it would be simpler to end things now.

A knock on the door heralded the arrival of his patient. Nick gratefully set aside his own problems while he dealt with him, but he knew that it was only a temporary reprieve. The situation wasn't going to go away because he chose not to think about it.

James Rogers was a good-looking man in his fifties, the director of one of London's largest firms of stockbrokers. HealthFirst offered a corporate healthcare programme whereby firms could pay a monthly fee so that key employees could receive private medical care. James was considering signing up his company for the scheme, and had put himself forward as the guinea pig to see how it worked. Today was the initial screening and health check which every employee would receive.

Nick ran through all the tests, checking the man's height, weight and body mass index, his blood pressure, cholesterol and an analysis of his urine and blood. He also tested James's cardiac and respiratory systems, his central nervous system and abdominal system, and carried out a test for bowel cancer because the man was over the age of forty-five. He rounded off the examination with a prostate screening and testicular check and was glad that he had when he found a small lump in one of the man's testicles.

'Had you noticed this swelling in your right testicle?'

'Yes, but I put it down to age.' James chuckled. 'One tends to develop all kinds of lumps and bumps as one gets older, I'm afraid.'

'That's very true.' Nick smiled, although he couldn't help wishing that the man had paid a little more attention to this particular lump. 'Have you experienced any pain at all, even some minor discomfort?'

'No, which is probably why I didn't take any notice of it,' James replied bluntly. 'What exactly are you suggesting, Doctor? Do you think there's a problem?'

'It's too early to say for certain,' Nick explained. 'There are several things which cause swelling in the testicles. It could be a fluid-filled cyst or even a varicose vein in the scrotum.'

'Or it could be something more serious, like cancer,' James suggested soberly.

'We can't rule out that possibility, although most swellings turn out to be benign, I'm happy to say. Why don't you get dressed and I'll talk you through your options from this point on?'

He left the patient to dress and went to his desk and made a note of his findings. James joined him a few minutes later, looking as immaculate as ever in his pinstriped suit.

'I would prefer it if you gave me the worst case scenario, Dr Slater,' he said firmly, sitting down. 'I'm not someone who likes to beat about the bush, mainly because I don't have the time.'

'Very well, then. If it is testicular cancer, it will need to be removed. The operation is called an orchidectomy and the surgeon will remove the diseased testis. The cure rate for that type of cancer is extremely good, between ninety-five and one hundred per cent if it's caught in its early stages.'

'I wouldn't mind getting returns like that on the stock market,' James said immediately.

Nick laughed. 'I'm sure you wouldn't. What I suggest is that I refer you to a specialist. He will carry out all the necessary tests and take you through the whole process. Do I take it that you would prefer to be seen privately?'

'Please. The quicker this is sorted out the better,' James agreed immediately.

Nick put through a call to a doctor they liaised with in Harley Street and made an appointment for the patient to be seen the following evening. James Rogers shook his hand warmly at the door when he saw him out.

'A very thorough examination, Dr Slater. I'm indebted to you for spotting a potential problem so soon. I shall be signing up my firm for the corporate scheme. Speed and efficiency are two things I value and it will be reassuring to know that key employees will have the benefit of your expertise.'

'Thank you. It's kind of you to say so, although I won't be here for much longer. I'm standing in for the clinic's director while he's away on leave,' he explained when James looked at him quizzically.

'Pity,' the man said bluntly. 'If I was in charge of this company, I would be doing my utmost to hang on to you.'

Nick went back to his desk after the patient left. There were a few more notes he needed to add to James's file.

It was good to know that he had been able to help, he thought as he jotted down a request for a copy of the test results to be sent to the Harley Street consultant. It made the job so worthwhile. It would be even better, of course, if he were able to follow through on the case and watch the patient making a full recovery.

The thought sneaked into his head before he could stop it, and he sighed. It had been a long time since he'd allowed himself to think like that. Not since he had abandoned his plans to join his parents' practice after Matt had died. He had told himself over the intervening years that it didn't matter if he never found out what happened to the people he treated, but it did.

He sank back in the chair, thinking about the decisions he'd made all those years ago, and what had prompted them. Discovering that Matt had Friedreich's ataxia had come like a bolt from the blue. The whole family had joked about how clumsy his brother was, but nobody had imagined it had been the inherited neurological disorder that had been causing it. It was only when Matt's speech had become affected that his parents had realised there had been something seriously wrong with him.

Nick felt a lump come to his throat as he recalled Matt's shock when he'd been diagnosed with the disorder. They had been in their first year at med school at the time and it had been hard for Matt to accept what the doctors had told him.

Friedreich's ataxia caused problems with balance, co-ordination and speech. Although not deemed terminal, difficulties with breathing and circulation often led to a sufferer's premature death. It had come as the cruellest of blows to a young man of nineteen.

The whole family had been sent for tests, which had proved that Nick's parents were both carriers of the gene that caused the disorder. Amazingly, Patrick, Helen and Penny were completely unaffected by it. However, the tests had shown that he was a carrier.

Nick took a deep breath. Although he knew he should be grateful that he wouldn't suffer like Matt had done, it had been a bitter blow. Being a carrier meant there was a chance that he could pass on the disorder to his own children. Although it needed both parents to be carriers of the defective gene before a child would exhibit the symptoms of Friedreich's ataxia, he couldn't rule out the possibility of it happening.

His own parents had married, unaware of the risks they'd been taking when they'd had their family. Admittedly, the chances of him falling in love with a woman who was also a carrier were slim, but it *could* happen. And even if any child he fathered didn't contract the disorder, he or she could still be a carrier and pass it on to future generations.

The thought that one day a child might suffer the same fate as Matt because of him was more than Nick could bear. That was why he'd decided that he could never have children and why he'd taken such care never to get involved in a relationship. It wouldn't be fair to any woman to deny her a family.

His heart ached as he made himself face up to the truth. No matter how he felt about Leanne, he had to stick to his decision rather than run the risk of hurting her.

CHAPTER FIVE

It was the longest morning of her entire life. Leanne could barely wait for one o'clock to arrive so that she could leave. She took care to avoid any situation which might mean her being alone with Nick, but the strain was enormous. She couldn't stop thinking about what she had overheard.

Had Nick deliberately set out to get her into his bed so that he could win that bet?

Part of her said that the idea was ridiculous, that he simply wouldn't do such a horrible thing, whilst another part said it might be true. After all, he could have found a few minutes to talk to her and try to straighten things out if he had wanted to. The fact that he seemed as eager to avoid her as she was to avoid him was the most damning proof of his guilt.

It was an effort to keep her mind on her work but she owed it to her patients not to allow herself to become distracted. She took blood samples and gave injections then took over the weight-loss clinic when Ruth Parker, another of the nursing staff, was held up dealing with a difficult patient.

HealthFirst offered several such clinics—smoking, impotence, fitness—but the weight-loss clinic was the most popular from all accounts. Careful checks were kept on people attending the clinic and advice was given about diet and fitness. The clinic employed its own dietician and fitness expert so guidelines were tailored to suit individual needs.

Heather Graham was a regular visitor to the clinic, according to her notes, but she didn't appear to be making any headway towards her goal of losing twenty pounds in weight.

'It's so hard!' Heather exclaimed as she stepped off the

scales. She was an attractive woman in her thirties, a high-flying businesswoman who travelled the world for the IT company for which she worked. She was beautifully dressed and made up, but it was obvious how unhappy she was about her inability to lose weight.

'I spend half my life on a plane so my body clock is all topsy-turvy. I end up having dinner when I really feel as though I should be having breakfast!'

'It must be difficult,' Leanne sympathised, jotting down the woman's weight on her chart. 'Do you carry your diet sheet with you when you travel abroad? It would help to have it on hand.'

'Yes, it's like my bible. I don't go anywhere without it.' Heather sighed. 'Mind you, it isn't a lot of use when I find myself in Scandinavia one week and the Far East the next. I'm eating things that I wouldn't have back home in London so I've no real idea about the number of calories they contain.'

'So it's a calorie-based diet you're following,' Leanne said, frowning.

'At the moment it is, although who knows what it will be next month? I've tried every diet known to man and none of them work.' Heather grimaced. 'I envy people like you who obviously don't need to watch what they eat.'

'I suppose I am lucky,' Leanne conceded. 'But it is luck rather than will-power. I love fresh fruit and vegetables so I naturally choose to eat things like that, although I'm not averse to the odd slice of chocolate cake, I must confess!'

'You and me both. That's the trouble. When I'm stuck in some hotel room on my own, I find myself phoning room service and ordering something sweet. It's a little treat for myself, you see.'

Leanne smiled because the truth was starting to emerge at last. 'It's probably those little treats that are causing the problem. If you could cut them out, you would soon find that you lost a few pounds. Once that happens it will spur you on to lose the rest. Why don't you phone a friend instead of ordering a snack? It might cost more, but it will be guaranteed free of calories.'

Heather laughed. 'I might just give it a go! A calorie-free phone call might be the answer to my problems. Anyway, thank you, Leanne. It's been good talking to you. I hope you'll still be here the next time I come in. The staff tend to change rather quickly so I'm never sure who I'll be seeing.'

'My contract is for three months,' she assured Heather as she walked her out. They said goodbye then Leanne went to see if there was anyone else waiting. She was just about to enter Reception when she heard Nick speaking to Ruth, who was manning the desk, and stopped because she didn't want to have to talk to him.

She went back to the treatment room and busied herself tidying up. However, she was very much aware that she couldn't keep avoiding him when they had to work together. How was she going to cope with the memory of what had happened last night hanging between them, though?

It made her wonder if she had been a little premature by telling Heather Graham that she would be working at the clinic for the next three months. The strain of being thrust into daily contact with Nick might become so great that she would be forced to find another job.

It was an unsettling thought and she couldn't help wishing that she'd been more sensible the night before instead of allowing her feelings to get the better of her. At least she had the consolation of knowing that she wouldn't end up like her own mother and find herself pregnant. That really would be the icing on the cake!

One o'clock arrived and Leanne collected her things in readiness to leave. She was planning on returning to the church in the village where her mother had lived to see if the young priest to whom she had spoken the previous day had found the parish records.

Apparently, they had been stored away when the church

had been re-roofed and he had promised to find them for her if she went back that day. She was just wondering if she should stop for something to eat before catching the tube to Camden Town when Melanie poked her head round the door.

'Nine o'clock in the wine bar on the corner, OK?'

'Sorry?' Leanne looked at her blankly.

'I'm having a leaving do tonight and I'd love it if you could come,' the other woman explained. 'We're all meeting at the bar. Sergio has organised everything and there will be nibbles and things.'

'Oh, I see. When you say everyone, who do you mean exactly?' she asked carefully. Although she appreciated the invitation, it seemed safer to find out if Nick would be there before she agreed to go.

'Sergio, Ruth, Robert, Natalie and Uma.' Melanie reeled off names. 'There's umpteen more coming but I can't remember everyone, to be honest.'

'What about Nick? Isn't he going?' she asked, turning to straighten her hair in the mirror so that Melanie couldn't see how much it hurt to say his name. Had he tricked her into his bed? Had he used her?

'No, he's got the wedding rehearsal tonight.'

'Wedding rehearsal? You mean he...he's getting married?' Leanne could hear the shock in her voice and knew that Melanie must have heard it too when she saw her frown.

'No, of course not. It's his sister who's getting married. Are you all right, Leanne? You've gone a really funny colour.'

'I'm probably hungry,' she said, forcing herself to smile, although the relief she'd felt on hearing that had almost made her keel over. 'I didn't have any breakfast and it's been too busy this morning to take a break.'

'Then go and have something now! That's an order.' Melanie glanced along the corridor and grimaced. 'Oops, we've got a queue again. I'd better go and do my bit even if it *is* my last day!'

Leanne managed to hold her smile until Melanie had left, but just thinking that Nick might have been getting married had been unbearably painful. She left the clinic but she knew that she wasn't ready to go to Camden while her head was in such a muddle.

She made her way instead to the café where she and Nick had had breakfast the previous day and bought herself a sandwich and a cup of coffee, hoping it would help if she had something to eat. She had been too on edge at the thought of seeing Nick to eat before she'd set off for work, and too upset after she'd overheard that conversation.

Had he lied to her, tricked her, played her for a fool?

Her eyes welled with tears as the questions came flooding back and the thought of eating the food she'd bought made her feel sick. She was about to throw it in the bin when a young girl approached her.

'If you aren't going to eat that, could I have it, please?'

'Of course.' Leanne handed over the tray then frowned as she took a proper look at the girl. She couldn't have been more than sixteen, with long, straggling brown hair. Her clothes looked as though she had slept in them and her hands and face didn't look too clean either.

Leanne had been shocked by the number of youngsters who slept rough on the streets of London and she had no doubt that this girl was one of them. What set her apart from the rest was that she was very obviously pregnant.

'If you're hungry I could get you something else as well,' she offered, touched by the girl's plight.

'No, this is fine. Thank you.' The girl gave her a shy smile then hurried away. As Leanne watched, she put the tray on a table then picked up the styrofoam cup of coffee and the sandwich and left the café.

Leanne followed her out to the concourse and watched as she found a quiet spot and sat on the floor to eat the food. She couldn't help feeling concerned because the girl looked so young to be on her own in that condition. She made up her mind to look out for her the next time she was in the station, although there was no knowing if the teenager would be there again.

At least the incident had helped to take her mind off her own problems, she thought as she made her way to the escalator to catch the tube. There were a lot of people in a far worse position than her. Maybe she should remember that and put what had happened last night behind her.

She sighed. It was a nice idea in principle but very difficult to achieve when every time she looked at Nick she would remember how she'd felt, lying in his arms.

The wedding rehearsal passed off smoothly, but Nick wasn't surprised. His sister Penny was always highly organised and had planned everything down to the tiniest detail.

The wedding was being held at the church in the village where his parents had their practice so he had dinner at home afterwards. He always enjoyed being with his family and he enjoyed it that night, too, laughing at the familiar old jokes and listening to his father regaling them with stories of life as a country GP thirty years ago. Nevertheless, he couldn't help noticing how tired his father and elder brother Patrick looked.

The practice was under increasing pressure now that a new housing estate was being built in their catchment area. They were desperately in need of another doctor, but so far they hadn't found anyone suitable and had made do with locums. Nick felt guilty because he knew that he could solve the problem if he agreed to join the practice, as his father and brother wanted him to do. It was what he and Matt had planned on doing before tragedy had struck and everything had changed.

He found himself thinking about the idea again as the conversation flowed around the room. However, it was the reason why he was now prepared to consider returning to Sussex that troubled him most. Thinking about the life he could have with Leanne if he settled down was tempting, but he had to remember that it wasn't simply a question of him moving back to Sussex and them living happily ever after. There were too many other factors that needed to be taken into account as well.

Frankly, it was a relief when the evening came to a close because it was painful to think about what he was missing out on. He gratefully accepted when Penny and her fiancé, David, offered him a lift back to London because it saved him a long and tedious train journey.

He kissed his mother, shook hands with his father and Patrick then made a hasty exit. Families were all well and good and he wouldn't be without his, but he needed some time on his own to get his head together. It was odd, then, how the minute Penny and David had dropped him off outside his flat and driven away he decided that being on his own was the last thing he felt like doing.

Nick checked his watch then hailed a passing taxi. Maybe he would be in time to join everyone for a last drink. It would be mean not to wish Melanie luck, he told himself as he slammed the cab door.

He sighed as the taxi roared off up the road. Who was he kidding? It wasn't Melanie he was interested in seeing but Leanne. Maybe it *would* be more sensible to leave things the way they were, but he couldn't bear to think that she believed he'd used her to win some stupid bet. He had to set matters straight between them if he did nothing else.

The bar was packed when he arrived so it took him a moment to locate the staff from the clinic. He spotted Robert first and waved when the young American let out a loud yippee.

'Didn't think you were going to show up,' Robert declared as Nick went over to join them. 'Don't tell me the wedding has been called off?'

Nick laughed. 'No chance of that. My sister has everything planned with military precision. Heaven help anyone who tries to upset her plans. It would need another world war to stop this wedding going ahead!'

'Cynic!' Melanie accused. 'It couldn't be that your sister

and her fiancé just happen to be in *lurv* and can't wait to spend the next fifty-odd years together?'

'I suppose that might have something to do with it,' he conceded, returning her grin although his heart was performing the most intricate kind of tap-dance. Leanne was sitting next to Melanie on the long banquette and he was so deeply aware of her that it was a wonder the rest of the group couldn't hear bells ringing.

He could hear them, and whistles blowing *and* see stars shooting—all the truly corny things that he had never believed actually happened in the real world. Shooting stars and ringing bells were the fodder of romance novels, he'd always firmly believed. But it just went to show how wrong a person could be.

He took a deep breath then turned to her and smiled, praying that he didn't look like a complete imbecile. 'Hello, Leanne.'

'Nick.' She afforded him the briefest acknowledgement before she turned to Sergio and said something to him.

Nick felt his nerves twist when he heard the handsome young Italian laugh. He turned away, fighting to control the emotions welling inside him. He *wasn't* jealous! He had no right to be. He had no claim on Leanne, just as she had no claim on him. If he repeated that often enough, surely he would believe it in the end?

'What's everyone drinking, then?' he said, striving for normality. He couldn't have been too far off the mark, thankfully enough, because nobody commented as they gave him their orders.

He went to the bar and ordered the drinks then waited while the barman poured them. There was a big, gilt-framed mirror on the wall and he found that if he positioned himself at the right angle he could see what was happening on the far side of the room…

He felt his heart jolt when he saw that Leanne was watching him. There was an expression on her face that made him want to cry all of a sudden. He couldn't recall ever having seen such pain in anyone's eyes before, and it hurt to know that he was the cause of it.

His hands were shaking as he carried the tray of drinks back to the table. Melanie grimaced as she picked up her dripping glass. 'Good job you aren't a surgeon, Nick. I wouldn't fancy my chances if you were operating on me!'

Everyone except Leanne laughed. Nick forced himself to join in as he unloaded the glasses, but his heart was aching. He didn't think he would ever forgive himself for having caused her so much distress.

'Don't worry, I know my limitations. Right, I don't know if anyone has proposed a toast yet, so I will. Here's to Melanie. May you find friends and happiness wherever you travel.'

Everyone raised their glasses and drank to the toast. Nick took a sip of his drink then looked round when Leanne suddenly stood up. She steadfastly ignored him as she turned to Melanie and smiled.

'Sorry to be a party-pooper, but I must go. I promised my dad that I would phone him and he'll be worried if he doesn't hear from me.' She bent and hugged the other woman. 'It's been fun knowing you, Mel. Take care of yourself.'

'You, too, Leanne.' Melanie returned her hug then turned when Ruth said something to her.

Nick moved aside to let Leanne pass as she came around the table. She gave him a nod of thanks then hurried to the door and not once did she look back at him. All of a sudden he knew that he couldn't leave things the way they were, couldn't bear to let her walk away and know that she would spend the night thinking the worst of him.

He put his glass on the table and ran after her, ignoring the demands from the rest of the party about where he was going. He didn't care what the others might think. He didn't care about anything except making Leanne see that it had been a horrible mistake.

He wrenched open the door in time to see her getting into

a taxi and swore in frustration. He knew which street she lived in but not the number of the house. Short of knocking on every single door he had no hope of finding her. He would have to leave things the way they were until tomorrow.

He sighed. Tomorrow seemed an awfully long way away.

Leanne took extra care with her make-up the following morning. She had spent a sleepless night and every wakeful hour showed in the dark circles under her eyes. A dab of concealer helped repair the damage, but nothing could put back the usual sparkle in her eyes. She felt flat and empty and no amount of titivating would alter that fact.

The queue for the tube was as long as ever and she kept looking over her shoulder, fearful that she would run into Nick again. In the event there was no sign of him, but it was worrying to realise how difficult it was going to be to work with him in the future. Once again the thought that she might have to find another job crossed her mind, but she knew that it wouldn't be easy to find one with such convenient hours.

The one good thing that had happened the previous day had been that the priest had found the parish records she needed. She was hoping to continue looking through the volume which listed all the marriages that had taken place in the church when she went back there that afternoon. Maybe she would find a mention of her mother in it.

She tried to hold on to that positive thought as she emerged into the station's concourse. It was frantically busy as usual and she had to wend her way through the crowds. She had just reached the stairs leading up to the clinic when a commotion broke out and she stopped to see what was happening. She could see someone lying on the floor, and it was a moment before she realised that it was the young girl to whom she'd spoken the previous day.

Leanne hurried over and pushed her way through the

crowd that had gathered. 'I'm a nurse. Please, let me through.'

She knelt beside the girl and checked her pulse, relieved when she felt it beating away. The teenager was unconscious. Her face was ashen and her skin felt clammy, all signs that she had fainted. Leanne was just trying to decide if she should call an ambulance when Nick appeared.

'What have we got?' he asked, crouching beside her.

'I think she's fainted,' she explained, trying to keep her tone as neutral as his had been. It wasn't easy, especially when he leant forward to gently roll back the girl's eyelids and their hands touched.

She heard him take a deep breath but his voice still grated when he spoke, hinting at the fact that he found the situation no easier to deal with than she did. 'I think you're right. How's her pulse?'

'A little fast, but nothing to be overly alarmed about,' she told him huskily.

He shot her a quick look and she couldn't fail to see the plea in his eyes. 'This isn't the time or the place, but we need to talk, Leanne. OK?'

'Yes,' she whispered, because she desperately wanted to clear things up.

'Good.' He touched her lightly on the hand then bent over the girl when her eyelids flickered. 'Just lie still for a moment. You might feel a bit woozy at first, but you're going to be fine.'

'Wh-what happened?' the girl began, before she suddenly closed her eyes again and groaned. 'I think I'm going to be sick!'

Nick glanced at Leanne. 'Let's get her upstairs. The last thing she needs is all these people watching her.'

'Of course.'

She scrambled to her feet while he picked up the girl. Dennis had opened up the clinic that day so they were able to take her straight to one of the treatment rooms and lay her on a couch. Leanne shed her coat then found a basin and put it on a stand beside the bed in case the girl was sick. She still looked very pale but her pulse was levelling off when Leanne took it again.

'She needs checking over. Can you get her out of that coat?' Nick's tone was grim as he took note of the girl's swollen abdomen. 'I doubt if she's been receiving any proper medical care. Who knows what problems it might have caused in her condition?'

Leanne knew he was right to be worried. She only wished that she'd had the foresight to do something more when she'd spoken to the teenager the previous day. She helped her out of her coat then found a sphygmomanometer and took her blood pressure.

'Her blood pressure's fine,' she exclaimed in relief. 'I was really worried that it might have been the problem.'

'So was I.' He checked the girl's ankles and lower legs and nodded when he found no signs of swelling. 'They look fine, too. I had visions of pre-eclampsia running through my head when I saw the state she was in.'

'Fortunately, it seems that we can rule that out,' she said, grimacing at that prospect.

Pre-eclampsia was a highly dangerous condition which sometimes occurred in pregnancy. It could lead to seizures and even death if it went untreated. A combination of high blood pressure, fluid retention and protein in the urine were the main symptoms of the disease, so it was good to know that it didn't appear to be the problem in this case, although Leanne would feel happier if they ran a complete series of tests on the girl.

Nick obviously thought so too because he turned to her. 'Can you take some blood samples? We may as well check everything is all right while we have the chance.'

'Of course.' She smiled reassuringly at the teenager. 'I'm just going to take some blood from you. It won't hurt so don't worry.'

'You aren't going to do anything else, are you?' The girl's

face contorted with fear. 'You won't do anything to hurt my baby!'

'Of course not. We just want to help you,' Nick reassured her, but Leanne could tell that he was as puzzled as she was by the remark. 'You don't need to be scared. Can you tell us your name?'

'If I tell you that, you'll tell my mum and dad.' The girl was becoming very agitated now. Leanne saw her look anxiously at the door, which they had automatically closed as they had a patient in the room with them.

Nick deliberately moved away from the bed and leant against the wall. She guessed that he was trying to make it clear to the girl that she could leave any time she chose to and that they wouldn't try to stop her.

'We won't do anything you don't want us to do. We only want to help you,' he explained gently. 'You don't have to tell us your last name, but it would help if we knew what to call you.'

The girl chewed her lip for a moment then shrugged. 'It's Amy.'

'Hi, Amy, it's nice to meet you. I'm Nick and this is Leanne. So, now that we've introduced ourselves, can you answer a few questions for me?'

'Depends,' Amy muttered.

'On what I ask you?' He laughed and Leanne saw Amy shoot him a wary look. It was obvious that the girl was trying to decide if she could trust him and Leanne found herself willing her to do so. Nick would do everything he could to help Amy if she would only let him. It was funny how certain she was of that fact when she'd been so uncertain about everything else for the past twenty-four hours.

'Well, don't worry because I have no intention of asking you any awkward questions,' he continued in the same reassuring tone. 'I'm not trying to find out where you live or how I can contact your parents, although if you want me to get in touch with them, I'll be happy to do so.'

'I don't,' Amy said quickly. 'I don't want them finding

out where I am because they'll only try to make me get rid of it.'

'You mean your baby?' he said gently. 'Did your parents not want you to have it? Is that why you ran away from home?'

'They said I was too young and that I had no idea the problems it would cause, but they don't understand!'

Amy knuckled away the tears and her expression was fierce all of a sudden. 'I couldn't kill it! That's what they wanted me to do when they found out I was pregnant. Mum said that she would arrange for me to have an abortion even though I told her it wasn't what I wanted. Then Dad said that if I didn't get rid of the baby I couldn't stay in the house. He was worried what the neighbours would think!'

Leanne bit back a sigh. What a nightmare it must have been for the family. If only they'd found a way to talk through the problem, surely they could have found a solution?

'People often say things in the heat of the moment that they don't mean, Amy,' Nick said quietly. 'Your parents probably regret what they said to you and wish they had the chance to straighten everything out.'

Leanne glanced at him when she heard the edge in his voice. Was he thinking about the fact that they needed to sort out their differences, perhaps? She sensed it was so and the weight in her heart seemed to lighten a little when she realised how important it was to him.

'The only way they want to sort things out is by making me get rid of my baby,' Amy retorted. She put a protective hand on her swollen abdomen. 'It's too late for that now, isn't it? I've only got another few weeks and the baby will be born.'

'Exactly how many weeks pregnant are you?' Leanne asked, forcing herself to concentrate on what was happening.

'Thirty-four, I think.' The girl coloured. 'I didn't go for a scan. The doctor gave me a note for the hospital, but I knew that Mum would find out if I stayed off school. She's the school secretary, you see, and she checks all the attendance registers.'

'How old are you, Amy?' Nick smiled when the girl's mouth pursed. 'And, no, you don't have to tell me, but it would help to fill in a few more details. The more we know, the more we can do to help you and the baby.'

'Sixteen.' She looked at him uncertainly. 'Do you really mean that about helping me? It's not a trick, is it?'

'No, it isn't a trick, love. I can make sure that you receive proper medical care from now on. I can also find you a place to stay until your baby is born if you want me to. It will be a lot safer than sleeping on the streets, which I imagine is what you've been doing.'

The girl sighed. 'It's not so bad during the day, but it can be scary at night. You never know what's going to happen then, which is why I try to stay in the station as long as I can. At least there are always people around in here.'

'What have you been doing for food?' Leanne queried, her heart going out to the girl. She couldn't imagine how hard it must have been for her in the past few months.

'People sometimes give me change if I ask them, and quite often there's food left on the tables in the cafés.' She grinned at Leanne. 'Although not many people throw away their whole lunch straight after they've bought it, like you did yesterday.'

'I don't imagine they do.' Leanne smiled, although she couldn't help noticing the frowning look Nick gave her. She had a feeling that he'd guessed why she hadn't eaten her lunch, and that it troubled him to know that it had been because of what had happened between them earlier that day.

It was an effort to confine her thoughts to the problem of convincing Amy to accept their help when she desperately wanted to clear things up between Nick and herself. 'Will you let us help you, Amy? I promise that you have nothing to be scared of.'

'If it means my baby will be all right, I suppose so.'

'Good. I need to check you over first, do some blood tests, things like that.' Nick went back to the bed and smiled at the girl. 'I imagine the reason you fainted was because you were hungry. Am I right?'

'I only had the sandwich and the coffee Leanne gave me yesterday,' Amy admitted.

'Well, you certainly need to eat more than that in your condition,' he said briskly. 'Let's give you the once-over then I'll get you something to eat and find you a bed for the night.'

Amy seemed resigned to letting them help her and didn't object. Leanne took the bloods for testing then Nick gave Amy a quick physical examination, listening to the baby's heartbeat and feeling its position in the girl's womb. He was extremely thorough and Leanne was impressed by his knowledge of antenatal care.

Nick was a good doctor, a caring one, too, she decided as she took the samples to the lab for testing. Could a man who cared so much about others really have set out to use her?

By the time someone arrived from the hostel to collect Amy, she had almost convinced herself that she'd been wrong about Nick's motives. However, there was still a tiny bit of her that needed to hear him tell her that she'd made a mistake. The trouble was, they were so busy that they never had a free minute all morning to talk.

When one o'clock rolled around, and it was time for her to leave, she was no nearer to resolving the problem. However, it seemed that Nick had his own ideas about how to remedy matters. She was on her way out of the clinic when he appeared. He was wearing his coat and he grinned when he saw her staring at him in surprise.

'I'm taking the rest of the day off. I've got umpteen hours owing to me and I doubt I'll get the chance to reclaim them before my contract runs out. Fancy some company this afternoon, Miss Russell?'

Leanne smiled back, feeling her heart lift with joy. 'Yes, please, Dr Slater.'

'Good.'

He didn't say anything else, but he didn't need to. Sometimes one word said more than several dozen could ever have done.

CHAPTER SIX

THEY took the tube straight to Camden Town. Neither of them was really hungry so there hadn't seemed any point stopping for lunch. As they exited the station, Leanne could feel her nerves tighten with anticipation.

At some point soon Nick would want to talk about what had happened and she wasn't sure what he would say. She was ninety-nine per cent certain that it would be what she hoped to hear, but there was still that one per cent of doubt in her mind.

They reached the church and he stopped and turned to her. 'Do you think we could clear up this misunderstanding first, Leanne?'

'I'd like that,' she agreed softly. She glanced over her shoulder and pointed to a bench just inside the gates. There was a graveyard in front of the church and she guessed that a lot of people had used the bench to sit and think about their loved ones over the years.

'Shall we sit there? It will be a bit quieter than trying to talk out here in the street.'

'Good idea.'

He followed her through the gates and with his usual courtesy waited until she'd sat down before sitting beside her. It was quite cold that day but the spot they had chosen was sheltered from the breeze. When he turned to face her, Leanne felt a flurry run along her nerves and bit back a sigh. If ever there was a moment when she didn't want to be aware of him it was now, when she needed to listen with her head, not her heart, to what he had to say.

'I never tried to get you to sleep with me to win that bet. It never even entered my head. What you overheard the other day was all down to Dennis's overly fertile imagination.'

'I'd hoped you'd say that, Nick,' she admitted. 'I suppose I jumped to conclusions, but it was such a shock to hear you two talking like that.'

'It was a shock for me when I saw you standing in the doorway, listening.' Nick took hold of her hand. 'I would never make a bet like that, Leanne, especially not when it concerns you. I...I care too much about you to treat what happened the other night as a joke.'

'Do you?' she said, her voice quavering despite all her efforts to remain in control. The past two days had been a nightmare and she couldn't stop her eyes filling with tears when she recalled the pain of believing that Nick had used her.

'Yes. I do.' He drew her into his arms and held her tightly so that she felt the shuddering breath he took. 'I care more about you than I've cared about anyone for a long time, Leanne. I made myself *not* care, if you can understand what I mean, but it's impossible to do that with you.'

The confession touched her deeply and she sighed. 'Oh, Nick, I don't know if it makes me feel better or worse to hear you say that. I can't help wondering why you've deliberately distanced yourself this way.'

'Because of what happened when Matt died. I made some decisions then and I have lived my life accordingly ever since. However, what I couldn't have allowed for was that I would meet you. I *do* care, Leanne, even though I know that we can never have a future together. I want you to remember that.'

'I shall,' she whispered, but her heart felt heavy once more.

Nick had ruled out the possibility of them continuing their relationship after her stay in England ended. Even though it was what they had both agreed initially, she couldn't help wishing that he would change his mind. After all, there was nothing to stop him going back to Australia with her, nothing to stop her staying in England for that matter. They were both free to choose what they wanted to do with their lives, but he had made his decision and it was final.

It was an effort to hide how painful she found the idea, but she knew it would be wrong to use any kind of emotional blackmail in this situation. She had no real idea why he was so determined to remain on his own, apart from the fact that it had something to do with his brother's death. However, if Nick had wanted to tell her anything else, he would have done so.

She gently withdrew her hands and stood up, forcing herself to smile when he followed suit. 'I'm glad we've got that cleared up. Let's forget about it now, shall we?'

'I hope we can, Leanne.' He took a deep breath and for a moment an expression of indecision crossed his face. She had a feeling that he was toying with the idea of saying something else, but in the end he thought better of it.

'So, what's next on the agenda? Is it time to start ploughing through a stack of dusty old parish registers?'

'How did you guess?' She deliberately kept her tone light, although she was intrigued to know what he'd been going to say. Had he been about to explain why he was determined to stay single for the rest of his life, perhaps?

It was an effort to put that idea out of her head, but she didn't want to spoil their newly restored harmony. 'Father Kenny has dug out the register of marriages and I was hoping that I might be able to find a mention of my mother in it. It's a bit of a long shot but she might just have got married in the church at some point after I was born. It's very slow work, though, because the entries are all handwritten and they're extremely difficult to read.'

'Well, I should have a head start on you there. You know what they say about doctors' handwriting so this should be a doddle!'

'Then what are we waiting for?' Leanne linked her hand through his arm and smiled up at him, feeling her heart skip a beat when he bent and dropped a kiss on her cheek.

'Thanks for being so understanding, Leanne,' he said softly, and there was an expression in his eyes that made her blood pressure shoot up a few dozen notches on the scale.

'You're welcome,' she murmured, leading him towards the church. She took a steadying breath as they went inside, but it was hard to ignore what had happened.

Nick wanted her. She had seen it in his eyes even though he hadn't said anything. The only problem was that there was a time limit on his need. He wouldn't want her after the three months were up, or if he did, he wouldn't do anything about it. She had to resign herself to the fact that all they had were these three months to be together.

It seemed very little when she wanted so much more.

Nick could tell how disheartened Leanne was when they closed the dusty old register. They had double-checked every entry, but they hadn't found any reference to her mother. He knew that she had been banking on finding something in the parish records and how disappointed she must be to have drawn a blank.

'What a shame,' he said sympathetically as they left the church after they'd thanked the young priest for his help. 'I was hoping we might find a lead.'

'Me, too.' She sighed as she pushed her hands into the pockets of her fleece jacket. 'I don't know where to go from here, to be honest.'

'There's always a chance that you'll find something when the Family Records Centre gives you access to your file,' he said, trying to sound encouraging. 'And isn't there a system whereby you can check to see if your birth mother has been trying to get in touch with you? I can remember reading something about it a few years ago, although I'm not sure how you go about it.'

He grimaced. 'One of the drawbacks of being out of the country all the time is that you get out of touch with how everything works.'

'You're not that far out of touch,' she assured him. 'It's called the Adoption Contact Register and I've already paid my entry fee and had my details added to it. Unfortunately, my birth mother isn't registered so it doesn't look as if she's been hoping for me to contact her.'

'Maybe she doesn't know about the scheme,' he said quickly, hating to see her looking so sad. 'A lot of times it's lack of knowledge that stops people doing something rather than the fact that they aren't interested.'

'I suppose you could be right,' she agreed as they walked back up the high street. It was still very busy, although a number of the pavement stall-holders were shutting up for the night. Camden was a very cosmopolitan area, a melting pot of all sorts of nationalities. Nick smiled as he caught snatches of conversation in a number of different languages.

'I know I'm right,' he said firmly. 'So don't start getting down in the dumps. Something will turn up soon, you'll see.'

'That's what I'm hoping.' She sighed wistfully. 'It might have been easier if my adoption had been handled by the local authority, but Dad told me that they'd had to go through a private agency because of Mum's health. It's crazy, all the silly rules they make up when people are trying to adopt a child, isn't it?'

'I suppose they try to do the best they can for the children in their care,' he observed lightly.

'Nobody could have had better parents than mine,' she said quickly.

'I'm sure you're right.' He stopped and turned her to face him, uncaring that they were blocking the pavement. All he was interested in was making sure that Leanne hadn't been hurt by his comment.

His heart lurched as he realised how important that was to him. He would fight dragons, walk a million miles, endure *any* hardship so long as she was safe and happy. If that wasn't love, what was?

'I'm sure your parents did everything possible for you.'

It was an effort to hide his dismay as that thought sneaked in, but it was Leanne's feeling that mattered most at the moment.

'They did. They were the best parents anyone could wish for. It probably sounds silly saying that when I'm looking for my birth mother, but it's true.'

'It doesn't sound silly at all,' he assured her as they carried on walking. 'And if I were in your shoes, I would feel exactly the same. Knowing about your background is important because it gives you a base to work from.'

He felt a spasm of pain run through him because that thought had hit home rather too sharply. His life might have been very different if he hadn't known about Matt's illness and the fact that he was a carrier of the gene that had caused it. It was an effort to rid his mind of the thought when Leanne continued.

'That's exactly how I feel. I would never wish for my life to have been different, but I need to know about the woman who gave birth to me.' She sighed. 'I want to understand how she could give me up because it's not something I could do.'

'Maybe she simply wasn't in a position to look after you and felt it was the right thing to do.' He put his arm around her and hugged her, knowing that she needed to feel secure at that moment, then wondered how on earth he could know that.

'That's what I keep telling myself.'

'And it's what you must try to hold onto.' He cleared his throat, afraid that she would wonder what was wrong with him if she heard the huskiness in his voice. He couldn't remember being so aware of anyone's feelings before.

'Having a child adopted is often the biggest act of love. If you can put the child's future happiness before your own needs, that really is a wonderfully caring thing to do.'

'I know you're right, Nick. Thank you for reminding me.'

Leanne reached up and kissed him on the cheek. It was just a light kiss but he couldn't even pretend how it made him feel. He turned her into his arms and kissed her hungrily, kissed her again tenderly, then let her go because the middle of a busy London street was hardly the best place to be giving in to this kind of temptation.

Leanne didn't say anything as they carried on walking. He had a feeling that she was finding it difficult to find the right words. How *did* they explain this desire they felt for each other, this need to have and to hold, to love and to cherish?

He had so little experience of feeling like this that he didn't know how to deal with it, didn't know even if he should try. Maybe there was a strong case for leaving things to work themselves out.

A shudder ran through him as he recalled what had happened the last time he had expressed that view. What had he called it at the time...going with the flow? They had ended up in bed together, but would it be right to let that happen again when he couldn't give Leanne anything apart from a few weeks of pleasure?

His heart ached because he knew that it could never be enough for either of them.

They arrived back at Euston in time to battle their way through the hordes of evening commuters. Leanne grimaced as a man running to catch a train nearly bowled her over.

'What a scrum! I've seen better behaviour on a rugby field.'

Nick laughed. 'Don't tell me you're into rugby?'

'Not really.' She grimaced as they made their way to the escalator. 'I'm not a fan of contact sports, full stop, although Michael used to drag me along to watch him play.' She wished she hadn't mentioned Michael's name when she saw Nick's mouth thin. She hurried on. 'How about you?'

'Rowing is more my sport, not that I get much chance to do any nowadays. I used to row for my university when I was an undergraduate and I grew to love the sport.'

'I suppose it's difficult to find the time when you're working,' she suggested.

'It's difficult to find a river more often, you mean.'

They had reached the top of the escalators and they automatically turned towards the exit as he continued. 'If you've ever tried finding a river in some parts of Africa where they've seen no rain for umpteen years, then you'll understand my problem.'

She laughed at the pithy comment. 'I can see how it might be difficult! So what do you do instead to keep fit? How about that bike I saw in your hall the other night? Do you go out for bike rides?'

'In this traffic?' He rolled his eyes as he looked along Euston Road. Leanne giggled because she could see what he meant. There were cars and buses queued up as far as the eye could see.

'I'd want danger money to ride a bike in London. No, the bike belongs to Penny. Her fiancé confiscated it a couple of weeks ago after she was knocked off it on her way to work. He asked me if I would store it in my flat until he could take it down to Mum and Dad's house. It's a bit quieter there, less chance of Pen getting flattened by a juggernaut,' he added with a grin.

'Did she object?' she questioned, enjoying hearing all these titbits about his family. Nick spoke about them so warmly that she knew she would like them if they met. She swallowed a sigh because the likelihood of that happening seemed very slim.

'No, because she believes the bike was stolen. David sneaked it out of their flat while she was at work.' He chuckled. 'It must be love if he's prepared to risk Pen's wrath when she finds out!'

'She'll forgive him,' Leanne stated firmly. 'After all, he was only doing it because he cares about her.'

'And that's how you would feel, is it, Leanne? You'd forgive someone if they did something behind your back so long as it was with your best interests at heart?'

'Probably,' she said thoughtfully. 'Of course, it all depends on what they did, but knowing someone cares about you makes a big difference, Nick.'

'Is that the voice of experience talking, by any chance?' He shrugged when she looked blankly at him. 'Michael must have been concerned about you, Leanne. I know you told me that he didn't want you to come to London because it meant his plans being disrupted, but I'm sure that was just an excuse. He was probably worried sick about you and that's why he raised so many objections. Have you forgiven him now?'

'At one time I would have done,' she admitted. 'I was so *besotted* by him that I would have convinced myself that Michael had only behaved that way because he cared about me.'

She gave a light laugh, wondering why it didn't hurt any more to talk about the man she had planned to marry. It seemed very odd until it struck her that it was because she had never really loved Michael. She had fallen for the image, not the man.

'Michael is handsome, witty, charming and very ambitious,' she continued, wondering why it had taken her so long to see that. She might never have realised it, in fact, if she hadn't come to London and met Nick. It was a deeply disquieting thought and she hurried on.

'He's a specialist registrar at the Royal Free in Sydney, where I worked, and he has big plans for the future. To be honest, I thought he was everything a woman could wish for until I discovered that he has one major flaw.'

'And what's that?'

She shot him a wary look when she heard the tightness in his voice, and felt her heart swell with tenderness when she realised that Nick was jealous of her relationship with Michael. He had no reason to be, she thought, because Michael wasn't half the man Nick was.

'Michael is pathologically selfish. It's in his genes. He

must be the only guy in the world whose DNA contains an extra strand for selfishness.'

She heard Nick roar with laughter and found herself joining in despite the fact that it worried her to have to admit how she felt about him. There was no future for them—as he had been at pains to tell her—but that didn't make any difference to how she felt. 'I mean it. Really, I do!'

'I know you do and I almost feel sorry for the guy.'

'Only almost?' she queried, feeling her pulse leap when he looked at her.

'He had you for however many months so I don't think he warrants too much sympathy. He has to be a complete fool to have let you go, Leanne. No plans are worth losing you for.'

'Does that mean you would change your plans, Nick?' She hadn't meant to say that, certainly hadn't intended to put him on the spot, yet she couldn't bring herself to tell him not to answer the question. She watched as an expression of pain crossed his face.

'I don't have any plans, Leanne. I never look beyond what's happening at this precise moment. There is no point wishing for things you can never have.'

There was something about the way he'd said that which made her heart ache. Why *was* Nick so determined never to plan for the future?

She had no time to work it out, however, because he suddenly took hold of her arm and steered her towards the pedestrian crossing as the lights changed.

'Where are we going?' she demanded as he hurried her across the road before the traffic could start moving again.

'I don't know about you but I'm starving. There's an Indian restaurant down this road which does absolutely the best curries this side of Bombay. Are your taste buds up to the challenge?'

'Them and me both!' she replied, deliberately adopting a cheerful tone because she knew that he wanted to change the subject.

It took them ten minutes to reach the restaurant and Nick kept up a lively conversation all the way there. She guessed that he was trying not to give her an opening to ask him any more awkward questions, but he needn't have worried. She would simply try to remember that there was a limit on their time together, and enjoy it while she had the chance. Not thinking about tomorrow was a habit she was going to have to get used to as well.

The meal was delicious. Nick knew that Leanne had enjoyed it every bit as much as he had done. They stayed in the restaurant long after the food had been eaten, just talking and enjoying being together. Although no mention had been made of it, he was aware that she was wondering what would happen once they left.

Did she expect him to invite her back to his flat? Was she thinking of inviting him to hers? Or had she decided that it would be wiser if they went their separate ways?

He paid the bill once it became apparent that the waiters were wanting to close for the night, adding a generous tip as compensation for having delayed them. Leanne went on ahead and he found her standing outside on the pavement, watching as her warm breath made puffy little clouds when it hit the ice-cold air. She turned and smiled at him and he felt his heart turn over when he saw the delight in her eyes.

'This is fun! Watch.' She sucked in a huge breath then blew it out, grinning like a six-year-old when it immediately froze. 'See!'

'Think that's good, do you? Well, watch this, young lady.' He took a deep breath then exhaled. 'Mine was bigger than yours!' he taunted.

'No way! If you call that a big one, mate, your eyes need testing.' She deliberately hammed it up by adopting a thick Australian accent. 'That's the trouble with you pommies. You've no idea what big really means!'

'Cheeky monkey! And after I just bought you dinner and treated you to several hours of my company, too.' His smile was teasing as he caught hold of her hand and pulled her to him. 'I think you owe me an apology, Miss Russell.'

Her lips were cool from the night air and lightly spiced from the meal they had eaten. Nick found that one kiss simply wasn't enough so he kissed her several more times. He might have continued doing so if the restaurant staff hadn't interrupted them as they left the building and started locking up.

He reluctantly let her go, sliding his arm around her shoulders as they headed down the street. He heard her sigh and looked at her quizzically. 'What was that for?'

'Because it's been such a wonderful evening and I don't want it to end.'

His breath caught so that it was a moment before he could say anything. 'It doesn't have to end if you don't want it to, Leanne.'

'I know. The problem is that I don't know if it's wise to get any more involved than we already are, Nick.' He heard her sigh again and there was a note of pain in her voice this time that cut him to the quick. 'It will only make it that much more difficult, won't it?'

'When we part, you mean?' His own voice sounded strained but there was nothing he could do about it. The thought of never seeing her again when she went home to Australia made him feel ill.

'Yes.' She turned to face him and her gaze was fierce all of a sudden. 'I could fall in love with you very easily, Nick Slater, but it would be a mistake, wouldn't it?'

He closed his eyes because he wasn't sure that he could trust himself to give her the right answer when she was looking at him with such hope in her eyes. All it would take was a few simple words and he could solve this problem, but it wouldn't be fair. He *couldn't* let her fall in love with him when he had nothing to offer her. He *had* to be strong!

'Yes, it would be a mistake, Leanne.'

He opened his eyes and tried to smile, but couldn't manage it when he saw the tears in her eyes. He drew her into his arms and held her tightly, wishing there was a better way to comfort her.

Holding her close and murmuring reassurances were all well and good, but they weren't what she wanted. However, the alternative—letting her fall in love with him—would be even worse. Leanne wanted children, and children were something he could never give her. How could he take her love then ruin her life by destroying all her dreams?

'I wish things could be different, sweetheart, truly I do,' he said, his voice grating as he tried to disguise the agony he felt. 'But I made up my mind about how I would live my life and I can't change it.'

'Can't or won't?' she queried, and he could hear the trouble she was having controlling her emotions. 'It isn't a sin to change your mind, Nick, neither is it a sign of weakness. I don't know why you decided that you want to spend your life on your own, but there is nothing *forcing* you stick to that decision.'

He shook his head because he simply couldn't risk explaining it all to her. He knew what would happen if he did, that she would be shocked at first, sympathetic later. She would tell him that he was being silly and that it didn't matter, but it did. He could never take the risk of having a child when there was a chance that it might be born damaged.

It was that thought which gave him the strength to hold fast to his resolve and she must have sensed that. She gave him a tight little smile as she stepped out of his arms and carried on walking.

Nick strode along beside her as she kept up a stilted conversation about the weather. It was a world away from the intimate mood that had developed over dinner and his impatience grew with every second that passed. He didn't want to be relegated to the role of a friend, but what choice did he have when he could never give her the commitment she deserved?

They reached her flat at last and Leanne stopped. 'Thank

you for today, Nick. I appreciate all the help you gave me this afternoon and dinner was wonderful. You must let me treat you next time.'

'Will there be a next time?' he asked before he could stop himself.

'I hope so. I couldn't bear to think that we won't be spending any more time together even though I think it's best if we stick to being friends rather than...' She hesitated then carried on, and he was overwhelmed by admiration for the fact that she didn't try to shirk the truth. 'Rather than lovers. That would be too big a strain for both of us, I think.'

'I'm sure you're right,' he agreed softly. He leant forward then stopped, wondering if he would be overstepping the new boundaries if he kissed her.

Leanne looked up at him with steady grey eyes. 'I think one last kiss is in order before we start being sensible, don't you?'

She moved towards him at the same moment as he bent so that their mouths met with a small jolt. Nick groaned when he felt his body instantly respond to the contact. Heat was surging along his veins in a tidal wave and his pulse seemed to have beaten itself right off the top of the Richter scale. It was an effort to draw back, especially when he saw how shaken Leanne was looking.

'I think I'd better say goodnight,' he said thickly.

'I think you should, too.' She half reached towards him then stopped when she realised what she was doing. 'Goodnight, Nick. And thank you.'

For what? he wanted to ask, only he wouldn't allow himself to ask that question. It wasn't her fault that they had found themselves at this impasse. It was his.

That thought certainly didn't make him feel any better. For the second time in a few short days, he found himself wondering if he was making a mistake by living his life this way. If he went back on the decision he had made after Matt had died then he could have everything a man could dream of having. He could have Leanne!

He half turned to go back and tell her that when common sense reasserted itself. Having what he wanted would come at a price, though. How could he risk Leanne's happiness?

'Try to relax, Mr Edwards. There's nothing to worry about. This won't hurt a bit.'

Leanne smiled reassuringly at the young man lying on the couch, but it was obvious how nervous he was. Daniel Edwards had arrived at the clinic shortly after they'd opened that morning, complaining of severe chest pains. Sergio had asked her to do an electrocardiogram to assess if there was anything wrong with his heart, and she was in the process of doing it. However, Daniel wasn't the most co-operative patient she had dealt with.

'This was probably a bad idea. I've a meeting in an hour's time and I can't be late.' Daniel swung his legs off the couch. 'I was hoping that you'd be able to give me some pills to take away the pain. I really don't have the time for this now. I think I'll leave it until another day…'

'Do you think that's wise?' Leanne put in gently. 'I don't want to scare you, Mr Edwards, but pains like the ones you've been experiencing need investigating sooner rather than later.'

'I'm only thirty-two!' he protested. 'I can't be having a heart attack at my age if that's what you're thinking.'

'I'm not. But it would be silly to take any risks when we can easily prove it one way or the other.' She picked up the electrodes and looked at him. 'It won't take more than fifteen minutes, I promise you. Surely you can spare that much time?'

'Oh, all right, then, if you insist.'

Daniel reluctantly lay down again. Leanne quickly attached the electrodes to various key points before he could change his mind and set the machine. Sergio would need to see a printout when he came back from dealing with another patient, and she wanted to have it ready for him to save time. She glanced round, expecting it to be him when the door opened, and felt her heart lift when she saw Nick coming into the room.

'Sergio has been held up,' he explained, drawing her aside. 'He asked if I'd take a look at this patient instead. Chest pains, I believe.'

'That's right,' she confirmed, trying her best to behave with the utmost decorum. It wasn't easy because being around Nick made it difficult to think about work, but she was too much of a professional to forget about their patient.

'I was just doing an ECG,' she explained, glancing at the machine as it began printing out its findings.

'Good.' Nick went to take a look, frowning thoughtfully as he studied the printed graph that showed the heart's activities as a series of spikes and dips. 'Everything looks fine to me. How long have you been having these pains, Mr Edwards? Sorry, I should have introduced myself. I'm Nick Slater, acting head of the clinic. Dr Alesi has been delayed with another patient so I hope you don't mind me taking over?'

'No, it's fine,' the young man answered quickly. 'I don't care who I see so long as you can get this sorted out as fast as possible. I've been having the pains for a couple of weeks now, but they've got worse in the past few days.'

Leanne tore off the printed strip and set it aside while the machine continued its tracings. She could see why Nick thought everything was fine because the reading showed that the heart's chambers were all contracting regularly and in sequence.

She smiled to herself when she saw him frown again as he considered what the patient had said. He wouldn't be rushed into making a decision despite how eager Daniel Edwards was to leave. Nick was very thorough and gave everything his due consideration.

That thought immediately reminded her of what had happened the previous night and she sighed. There was no escaping the fact that Nick had given a lot of thought to his decision to remain solo and she couldn't help wishing that she knew the reason behind it.

She had spent another restless night, wondering if she had done the right thing by telling him that she thought they needed to cool their relationship. Even though Nick had agreed with her, she knew that he would find it as difficult as she did. Their feelings for one another wouldn't go away because they had placed a limit on them. She wanted him more than ever, knew that he wanted her, too. But she didn't want to leave England in a few weeks' time with her heart in tatters.

It was a depressing thought and she drove it from her mind as she moved to the bed to hear what Nick was saying.

'Do you suffer these pains particularly after strenuous exercise?' he asked the patient.

Daniel shook his head. 'No. I don't get the chance to exercise nowadays. I spend most of my time stuck in front of a computer. I set up a dot com business last year, selling high-quality shoes and bags. It's been a nightmare.'

'Really?' Nick's tone was bland, inviting confidences, and the young man responded to it immediately.

'Yes. It seemed so easy at first, but funding has been my biggest headache. One of my major backers has just pulled out and it's caused no end of problems.'

'And you've been feeling the pressure, I expect.' Nick smiled when Daniel nodded. 'What other symptoms have you experienced? Breathlessness? Feelings of panic and a fear that you can't cope?'

'Yes, but how did you know?' Daniel asked in amazement.

'Because they're all classic symptoms of stress. In a nutshell, Mr Edwards, the pressure you've been under lately is causing the pains in your chest and all the other symptoms as well.'

'You mean that they're all in my mind?'

'Not at all,' Nick assured him. 'Stress and anxiety can cause very unpleasant physical side-effects.'

'So what's the answer? I'm not sure if I fancy loading myself up with a lot of pills,' Daniel said uncertainly.

'Drugs only help to alleviate the symptoms. They don't cure the underlying cause of the problem.' Nick's tone was firm. 'You need to reassess your lifestyle and take steps to reduce the amount of pressure you're under, even though I realise how difficult it will be.'

'At the moment I could happily throw in the towel and go off beach-combing,' Daniel admitted with a flash of black humour. 'There wouldn't be much stress in that!'

Nick laughed. 'That might solve your problems in one fell swoop, although it's rather a drastic course of action. My advice is to cut down your workload and learn how to delegate.'

'No chance of that at the moment,' Daniel observed glumly. 'If I don't pull out all the stops and find some extra funding, the company will close.'

'Then ask yourself what you really want from life,' Nick said quietly. 'It's up to you to decide if you're happy, living the way you're doing.'

Leanne glanced at him when she heard the edge in his voice. Had Nick been doing that, she wondered, thinking about what he wanted from life?

She sensed it was so and also guessed that the reason he had been giving it so much thought was because of her and the way they felt about each other. As she saw Daniel Edwards out a short time later, she found herself uttering a silent prayer that Nick would realise what a mistake he was making by denying them the chance of finding happiness together.

All it needed was for Nick to realise what he was in danger of losing.

CHAPTER SEVEN

THE days flew past, and before Nick knew it the week of his sister's wedding had arrived. Penny had asked him to be one of the ushers so there were fittings for a top hat and tails to squeeze in after work.

In a way it was a good thing that he was kept so busy because he had a legitimate reason for limiting the amount of time he spent with Leanne. They went for a drink one night, and she insisted on treating him to a meal another time, but they deliberately kept things low-key and he was grateful for that.

He'd had several sleepless nights after he'd spoken to Daniel Edwards about the changes the young man needed to make to his life. It made him feel like a hypocrite to have offered advice like that. He was very aware that *he* needed to make some decisions, but the thought that he might end up hurting Leanne was too painful to contemplate.

He went to collect his suit during his lunch-break the day before the wedding and arrived back at the clinic to find Leanne manning the reception desk. She was working afternoons that week because the nurse who usually worked that shift had left without giving any notice.

Nick smiled as she got up and opened the door when she saw him struggling with the suit carrier and the box containing his top hat. 'Thanks. I don't know how all those mums manage, hauling around buggies and kids. Just negotiating the escalators with this little lot was a nightmare!'

'I can imagine.' She smiled and he felt his heart give its usual little lurch when he saw the warmth in her eyes. Although they'd made every effort to keep their relationship on a platonic footing, it hadn't changed how they felt. It made him feel all knotted up inside to see the proof of that now.

'So it's the big day tomorrow,' she observed as she went back to her seat. 'Is your sister very nervous?'

'Not a bit.' He dumped the hat box on the desk and grinned at her, loving the way her eyes immediately lit up. 'I don't know how Penny will be on the actual day, of course, but she's fine at the moment. And so is David, amazingly enough.'

'That's good to hear. Is it a big wedding or just close family and friends?'

'Huge, from what I can gather. Pen seems to have invited the world and his wife!' He grimaced when she laughed. 'I'm not kidding. I only hope that Dad has hired a big enough marquee to fit everyone in.'

'Your parents are having the reception at their house?'

'Yes. Mum and Dad have this huge house, far too big for them now that we've all left home. There's plenty of room for guests to stay overnight so long as they don't mind sharing.'

'Sounds like fun. It must be great, being part of a big family,' she observed wistfully.

'Hectic, I'd call it,' he replied, hating to see her looking even the slightest bit sad. 'I don't know how Mum coped when we were younger. We got up to all sorts of mischief, but nothing seemed to faze her.'

'I'd love a big family. I suppose it's because I was an only child.' She laughed. 'I can only think of the advantages rather than the drawbacks!'

'And there are plenty of those,' he said, deliberately keeping his tone light.

He picked up the box, trying his best to blot out the image that had sprung to mind. It would serve no purpose, letting himself dwell on the thought of how beautiful Leanne would look when her body was swollen with child, no point tormenting himself because he wouldn't be the father of her baby. He couldn't and wouldn't run the risk of bringing a child into the world.

'I'd better make a start,' he said, trying to curb the pain that thought had caused him. 'Is there anyone waiting to be seen?'

'No. It's been really quiet. Sergio has a woman in room one and someone phoned to ask if they needed an appointment, but that's all.'

Her tone was perfectly level, but Nick could hear the undercurrent it held. Leanne had picked up on his pain and was wondering what had caused it. It hurt all the more to know that she was so sensitive to his feelings.

He made his way to his office and hung up the suit then stowed the hat box in a corner. There were some notes he needed to write up so he went to his desk. However, after a few minutes of sitting there with his pen poised above a blank sheet of paper, he gave up.

Tilting back his chair, he let his mind drift off towards the future and what he had to look forward to. He had been planning on going to South Africa after he left England. The agency that arranged his placements had told him that they were desperate for experienced doctors to work there. He had been looking forward to it, but now the thought of going to a completely different continent to the one where Leanne would be living made his insides spasm with pain.

He didn't want to be that far away from her, but it wouldn't be fair to change his plans and go to Australia with her. It would only prolong the agony for both of them. It would be better if they made a clean break as soon as her stay in England ended.

A stabbing pain pierced his heart because he knew how difficult it was going to be to let her go.

It was a busy afternoon after the slow start. At one point they had six people waiting. Nick phoned the administration department and asked for one of the office staff to man the desk while Leanne dealt with patients.

She took bloods for testing, gave umpteen vaccinations to guard against various tropical diseases then attended to an old lady who had fallen whilst getting off the escalator and cut both her knees.

Normally, they wouldn't have dealt with something like that because the poor soul obviously couldn't afford to pay for treatment. However, Nick bent the rules after the woman's anxious husband brought her into the clinic, and told Leanne to treat her without making a charge. She had no idea how he would square it with the company, but she applauded his decision. Money came a poor second to someone's health.

She was getting ready to leave at eight o'clock that evening when the door opened and a young woman came hurrying in.

'Can I help you?' she asked politely, hoping that it wouldn't be anything too complicated. Most of the staff had gone home and there was just her and Nick left in the clinic. He was dealing with another late arrival.

'Is Nick still here, by any chance? I'm Penny, his sister. Maybe he's mentioned me?'

'He has indeed. Congratulations! I believe you're getting married tomorrow,' she declared warmly, immediately spotting the resemblance. Penny had the same dark hair and wonderful smile as her brother, although there was a decidedly rueful twist to it at that moment.

'I thought I was, but now I'm not so sure.' She sighed when Leanne looked at her in surprise.

'David, my fiancé, has only gone and broken his ankle. He tripped over some steps on his way out of work this evening and—bingo! And, as if that wasn't enough, his best man has just phoned to say that his flight from New York has been delayed. He won't be landing at Heathrow until well after midnight now.'

'Oh, no! What rotten luck,' Leanne exclaimed. 'Look, I'll go and tell Nick that you're here. He's got a patient with him, but he shouldn't be long.'

'Thanks.' Penny sank onto a seat and Leanne could see tears welling into her eyes. 'It was all going so well, too. Now I don't know what's going to happen. I've got to get to Sussex and Gareth will need to be collected from the airport. We've only got the one car and David can't drive with his ankle in plaster.'

'It will be fine, you'll see,' she said quickly, coming round the desk and giving Penny a hug. 'Nick will think of something.'

She hurried to his office and tapped on the door. His patient was almost ready to leave and he smiled when he saw her. 'I won't be long if you've got someone else for me.'

'It's your sister,' she explained, motioning for him to step outside while she told him what had happened. He sighed when she'd finished recounting everything that Penny had told her.

'I thought things were going too smoothly. Tell Pen I'll be there as soon as I can, will you, Leanne? And try to keep her calm.'

'Will do.'

She hurried back to Reception and found Penny crying her eyes out. 'Hey, come on, now. There's no need for that. We can work something out. Where is your fiancé at the moment?'

'Back at the flat, feeling very sorry for himself.' Penny accepted the tissue Leanne gave her and dried her eyes. 'Thanks. I know it's stupid to get so upset but the logistics are a nightmare. We were all supposed to be travelling down to Sussex together. David and Gareth had booked a room at the village pub for the night, but now I don't know what's going to happen.'

'It will all work out,' Leanne assured her again, although it did seem as though they were going to have problems.

Leanne stayed with her until Nick had finished with his patient then went to fetch her coat. Frankly, she couldn't imagine how they would work everything out. From the sound of it they might end up spending most the night driving up and down the country.

Penny looked more upset than ever when she went back to Reception, and Leanne's heart went out to her. Without stopping to consider if she might be interfering, she went over to her. 'Look, if there is anything I can do to help, just say so.'

Nick looked up at her and smiled. 'Do you really mean that?'

'Of course I do! I don't say things I don't mean.'

She saw his eyes darken and bit her lip. Was he remembering all the things she had told him about how she felt? she wondered, and knew it was true. It was an effort to concentrate when he carried on speaking.

'In that case, we would love you to help, wouldn't we, Pen?'

Leanne saw his sister glance sharply at him before she smiled. 'Of course. But what have you got in mind?'

'If Leanne drives down to Sussex with you in your car then I can hire another car and collect Gareth from the airport. I know how you hate driving on your own at night so it will solve that problem. I'll spend the night here in London with David and Gareth, and drive them down to Sussex first thing in the morning. At least this way we'll all get a few hours' sleep.'

'What a brilliant idea!' Penny beamed as she turned to Leanne. 'And that way you get to come to the wedding, too, which is even better.'

'Oh, but I couldn't. I mean, it's far too late to invite another guest,' she began, but Nick quickly interrupted her.

'Rubbish! It's a buffet lunch so you won't be ruining any elaborate table plans, if that's what you're worried about. Plus Mum and Dad would love to meet you.'

He took a deep breath, but his voice seemed to grate when he added, 'And I would love it if you could be there, Leanne. It would make the day even more special.'

Leanne knew that Penny was hanging onto every word,

but there was nothing she could do about it. She felt her whole body suffuse with heat when she saw the way Nick was looking at her. There wasn't a doubt in her mind that he had meant what he'd said, and suddenly she couldn't find it in her heart to refuse.

'So long as you're sure that I won't be causing any problems, I'd love to come. Thank you.'

'Good.' Nick smiled back, but she saw a fleeting uncertainty cross his face. He knew as well as she did that spending the weekend together would be a test of their resolve to keep their relationship on a purely platonic footing.

Just for a moment she found herself wondering if she was a fool to put herself in such a difficult position, but there was no way that she could back out now that the arrangements had been made, neither did she really want to. Maybe it *was* madness, but the thought of spending a whole weekend with Nick was too tempting to resist.

She followed Penny from the clinic and waited while Nick locked up. They caught the tube together, but Nick and Penny stayed on the train so they could go back to Penny's flat and tell David about the change of plans. Penny had promised to collect her later so Leanne had half an hour to pack an overnight bag.

She waited on the platform for the train to leave, and the last thing she saw before it roared away into the tunnel was Nick smiling at her. She hurried to the escalator, trying not to think too much about what was happening. She was just going to spend the weekend in the country with friends. If she viewed it simply as that then there wouldn't be a problem.

Her heart gave a small hiccup of incredulity.

If she believed that, she would believe anything!

Traffic was light when they drove out of London the following morning at a little before six. Nick was grateful for that. It had been some time since he had driven in England and it took him a while to get used to being on the left-hand side of the road. Fortunately, David and Gareth were too hungover to notice any mistakes in his driving so didn't comment.

He sighed when he heard loud snoring coming from the back seat where his brother-in-law-to-be was reclining. Pen would kill him if she found out that he hadn't kept a closer eye on her beloved. It was just that he had been somewhat abstracted last night, and hadn't realised that David and Gareth had made enthusiastic inroads into a bottle of duty-free Scotch. His mind had been too full of thoughts of Leanne to babysit the pair.

Nick felt his heart lift and deliberately tightened his grip on the steering-wheel. He couldn't afford to let his mind wander even if the traffic wasn't all that heavy. Thinking about Leanne seemed to push all other thoughts from his head, and Pen certainly wouldn't thank him if he ruined her big day by ending up in a ditch.

He managed to keep his mind on the job until they reached the village. As he turned into the courtyard of the pub where David and Gareth had been due to spend the night, he found himself wondering if Leanne was up. It was barely eight o'clock and he wouldn't blame her if she had taken the opportunity to lie in.

All of a sudden his mind was awash with pictures of her lying in bed. Her glorious red hair would be spread across the pillows and her eyes would be closed. His mind took the scene a stage further and suddenly there he was, too, kissing her awake, his hands caressing her beautiful body...

He pulled into a parking space with a screech of tyres and Gareth, who had been dozing in the passenger seat, looked at him in alarm.

'Sorry. My driving's a bit rusty.' Nick turned off the engine then quickly got out of the car and sucked in several deep lungfuls of cold morning air in the hope they would cool him down.

They didn't work.

He wanted Leanne so much that it hurt! He wanted to

touch her, hold her, kiss her and make love to her. He also wanted to be with her now and for all the years to come, and that was the scariest feeling of all. He might be able to satiate his desire for her beautiful body in time, but how did he satisfy feelings like that?

He wanted everything that made a *real* relationship, all the bad times as well as the good. He wanted her in a hundred different ways and for a hundred different reasons, but not one of them was enough to justify him acting upon his feelings. What it all came down to was what did he really have to offer her?

True, he could love her more than any woman had been loved before, but he was under no illusions that it would be enough. Leanne had made no secret of the fact that she wanted a family and that was the one thing he could never give her. What right did he have to spoil her dreams?

Surprisingly, Leanne had slept well so that it was a little after eight when she awoke to find the sun streaming in through the window. It was such a rare treat to see it that she thought she was back in Sydney for a moment before her mind leapfrogged her forward in time and place.

She wasn't in Sydney but in Sussex and not just anywhere in Sussex, too. She was in Nick's bed, in his room, at his parents' house. So how did that make her feel? Scared? Excited? A bit of both?

She sat up and looked around the sunlit bedroom, taking her time as she took stock of the books piled haphazardly in the bookcase, the dusty collection of model planes arranged on a shelf above the desk, the display of tarnished sporting trophies in a glass-fronted case.

Nick must have been into rock music at one stage and the fading posters of leather-clad guitarists that peppered the walls made her smile. It was like looking at a series of snapshots of his life as he had been growing up, a procession of links from the boy he had been to the man she loved.

The thought flowed into her head so gently that it caused

barely a stir, and she sighed. She had tried to stop herself admitting how she felt about him but what was the point? She loved him and she may as well accept it. That he loved her, too, was something she wouldn't think about because it was too painful. Even if Nick *did* love her, he would never act upon his feelings.

It was an effort to shake off the feeling of melancholy that thought had caused, but this was Penny's day and she didn't want to spoil it. She showered and dressed then went downstairs to see if she could help.

Nick's mother greeted her warmly when she went into the kitchen. It had been very late when she and Penny had arrived the previous night and there had been all sorts of explanations to get through about the change in plans.

Leanne had done little more than introduce herself to Nick's parents before it had been time for bed. She felt somewhat guilty about turning up uninvited, but it soon became clear that Louise Slater wasn't in the least bothered about having an extra guest to stay.

'Come in, my dear. There's coffee in the pot and bread in the bin so help yourself to toast if you want some.' Louise laughed lightly. 'I hope you weren't put off by all that clutter in Nick's room and managed to get some sleep. Those dreadful old posters he insists on keeping are enough to give you nightmares!'

'I slept really well, thank you.' Leanne smiled as she poured herself a mug of coffee then popped some bread in the toaster. 'It takes more than a few posters to scare me!'

'Good.' Louise patted the chair beside her. 'Now, sit down and tell me all about yourself. Everything was so chaotic last night that we didn't get a chance to talk. Penny told me that you work with Nick at the clinic?'

'That's right.' Leanne felt a little colour warm her cheeks when she saw the speculation in the older woman's eyes. It was obvious that Louise had been adding two and two, and she wasn't sure what answer she had come up with. Exactly how *did* she explain her relationship with Nick?

'I had a feeling there was something going on when he came for dinner the other week,' Louise said cheerfully. She got up to top up her coffee and smiled at Leanne. 'He seemed very edgy, which isn't at all like him. I do hope this means that he's seen sense at last?'

'I'm sorry?' Leanne looked at her uncertainly and Louise sighed.

'Nick has spent his adult life avoiding commitment. I know why he's done so, of course, but I've always hoped that he would come to terms with what happened eventually.'

'Do you mean his brother's death?' Leanne said carefully, not sure if it was right to discuss Nick behind his back, even though she desperately wanted to hear what Louise had to say.

'Yes. Although it wasn't just Matt dying, of course…' Louise stopped as the back door opened. Her face broke into a rather guilty smile when Nick came in. 'Hello, darling, so you made it here all right in the end?'

'Just about.'

He came into the room and draped the suit-carrier over a chair while he kissed his mother's cheek. Leanne felt her heart flutter when he turned to her next. The kiss was no more than a token, yet she could feel the blood pounding through her veins when he straightened, knew that he was feeling exactly the same when she saw the expression on his face. It was only when Louise pushed back her chair that she realised they had been staring at one another for several seconds.

'I'll go and tell Penny that you're here, darling. It will help to settle her nerves if she knows that David has arrived safely.' Louise treated them to a knowing smile as she went to the door. 'There's nobody else up yet so you won't have anyone coming in and *disturbing* you.'

Nick sighed as his mother carefully closed the kitchen door behind her. 'Mum is a love, but subtlety has never been her strong point, I'm afraid. Sorry about that.'

'It's OK.' Leanne forced herself to smile but it was difficult to hide how uncomfortable she felt. Louise had obviously sensed something was going on and she wasn't sure what to do about it. She jumped when Nick pulled out a chair and sat down.

'Has Mum been grilling you?' he asked ruefully.

'Not at all. She's been lovely,' she assured him. 'Not many people would cope as well with having an extra guest turn up as she has done.'

'Oh, Mum takes it all in her stride. She got used to us bringing friends home to stay. Most weekends the house was packed to the rafters.'

'It was the same when I was growing up. Our house was always full of my friends. Mum and Dad loved having children in the house and never minded how many people I invited home. I think they were sorry when I got too old for sleep-over parties, in fact!'

'That takes me back.' He laughed. 'Matt and I used to have this huge tent in the garden and all our friends would come over and sleep in it with us. We once managed to cram ten of us in, would you believe? We were like sardines!'

'It sounds like you had a lot of fun,' she said, smiling at him.

'We did.'

There was a wistful note in his voice that tugged at her heart. Without stopping to think, she reached across the table and touched his hand. 'I hate it when you look so unhappy, Nick. I wish there was something I could do to help.'

She heard him take a deep breath before he turned his hand over and captured hers. Raising it to his lips, he pressed a kiss to her palm and his eyes were very green and very warm when he looked at her. 'Just being around you helps, Leanne. It makes me feel as though the world is a better place.'

'Does it?' she asked, her heart racing because of the way he was looking at her, with such tenderness, such need. Was it possible that he loved her? she found herself wondering giddily.

'Yes.' He gave her fingers a last, gentle squeeze then stood up. And it was as though he was deliberately withdrawing from her. 'I'd better take this little lot upstairs before it ends up with coffee spilled all over it. Pen will kill me if I turn up at the church looking a sight.'

'Of course.'

It was an effort not to show how hurt she felt. She gathered together the dirty dishes and took them to the sink to avoid having to look at him. Every time Nick realised he was getting too close to her, he took a deliberate step back. It almost broke her heart to know there was nothing she could do about it.

'I'll wash these dishes then see if your mother needs a hand,' she told him, praying that he couldn't hear the ache in her voice.

'I'm sure she'll appreciate it.' He opened the door then paused to look back. 'I'm glad you're here, Leanne.'

'Are you?' This time there was no way that she could disguise the catch in her voice.

'Yes. When I remember this day it will be all the more special because you were here to share it with me.'

He didn't say anything more and she was glad that he didn't. She didn't think she could have listened without breaking down. She ran water into the sink and washed the dishes, and it was only when she went to find a towel to dry them that she realised the moisture on her cheeks was tears, not splashes of dish-water.

There was no doubt in Nick's mind that all he would have in the future were his memories because he had ruled out the possibility of them being together. She had known how he felt all along and yet it still hurt to have to face the truth.

Even if Nick did love her, he would never change his mind about them being together.

CHAPTER EIGHT

THE wedding was due to take place at eleven o'clock, but Leanne had barely finished tidying the kitchen when the van delivering the flowers arrived, closely followed by the caterers, who wanted to start setting up the tables in the marquee for the reception.

She helped all she could by ferrying the table arrangements down to the marquee and phoning the florist to ask where the buttonholes for the ushers were when Louise discovered that they weren't in the box with the rest of the corsages. It was all very hectic, especially when Nick's eldest sister, Helen, arrived with her husband and children.

Helen sent the girls upstairs to see Penny, handed over the baby to her husband then settled down to give Leanne a grilling. It was all done in the nicest possible way, but it was obvious that Helen wanted to know exactly what Leanne's connection was to her brother. Leanne did her best to explain it and breathed a sigh of relief when Helen appeared to accept that she and Nick were just friends, even though she knew that it came nowhere near describing their relationship.

At ten o'clock she went to get ready, hoping that the burgundy crêpe dress she had brought with her would be suitable. Louise had insisted on lending her a hat, and had left it on the bed ready for her. Leanne had never worn a hat like it before and wasn't sure if the elegant confection of polished black straw, with its tiny spotted veil, would suit her. However, she didn't like to hurt Louise's feelings by refusing to wear it.

She showered and dressed then pinned her hair into a knot on the crown of her head and did her make-up, outlining her eyes with soft grey pencil and darkening her lashes with an extra coat of mascara. She studied her reflection in the mirror and realised there was something missing. What she needed was some lipstick to do justice to the elegant hat so she applied a soft, wine-coloured lip-gloss then put on the hat and carefully adjusted the veil. She had to admit that the effect really was rather stunning.

There was nobody about when she arrived downstairs so she went into the sitting room to wait. Louise was helping Penny get ready while Helen was busily organising her three small daughters, who were to be bridesmaids. Leanne could hear a lot of laughter coming from upstairs and smiled wistfully. If and when she ever got married there would be hardly any family to attend on her big day.

Her search for her birth mother had led nowhere. She had finally seen her adoption file at the Family Records Centre, but all it had contained was the same address in Camden that was listed on her birth certificate. She'd hoped that there might have been some kind of personal message from her mother in the file, but there hadn't been anything else.

She'd decided to try a different approach and had spent several afternoons at the records centre, checking the indexes to the births, marriages and even deaths in the hope that she might be able to find some trace of Mary Calhoun in them. However, once again she had come up with nothing. As the clerk who had helped her had gently explained, their records covered only the registers for England and Wales. If her mother had been living elsewhere, they wouldn't have her details on file. Although Leanne hated to admit, it looked as though she might never find her.

It was such a poignant thought that she sighed as she went to the window and looked out across the gardens. She had come to London with the sole intention of finding out about her birth mother. She'd never dreamed that she would fall in love while she was here. Now it looked as though she would be returning to Australia in a few weeks' time, knowing no more about the woman who had given birth to her *and* with her heart broken. She couldn't help wondering if she should have heeded everyone's advice and not made the journey to England. Surely she would have been better off if she'd never met Nick?

'So here you are. I was wondering where you'd got to.'

The sound of Nick's voice made her turn and she felt her heart swell when she saw him standing in the doorway. He looked so handsome in the tailed suit, she thought. The cut of the jacket emphasised the width of his shoulders and the narrowness of his waist, made the most of his height and bearing. He was wearing a gold brocade waistcoat and cravat under the jacket, and the colour brought out the golden glints in his hazel eyes.

Leanne just stood and stared at him, wishing she could bottle this moment and take it away with her when she left. All of a sudden she knew that no matter what happened she *didn't* regret having met him. Everyone needed to experience a love as deep and as all-consuming as the one she felt for Nick once in their lives.

'I haven't got a smut on my nose, have I?' He laughed as he ran an exploratory finger down his nose.

'No. I'm staring because you look so handsome,' she said, smiling at him with her heart in her eyes.

'I was just thinking the same about you,' he said softly. He crossed the room and took hold of her hands. 'You look beautiful, Leanne. That dress is gorgeous and the hat is perfect.'

His gaze skimmed over the shiny black straw hat with its coquettish little veil before it came to rest on her mouth, and she felt her skin prickle with awareness when she saw his eyes darken.

'You're even wearing lipstick,' he said, his deep voice throbbing slightly. 'I don't think I've ever seen you wearing it before.'

'I stopped wearing it because Michael said that it made my mouth look too big,' she told him, feeling her limbs turning to liquid as he continued to study her.

'He must be an even bigger idiot than I thought,' he said gruffly, his eyes tracing the contours of her mouth in a way that made her stomach knot and her lips go dry. Instinctively, the tip of tongue snaked out so that she could wet them and she heard him groan as he pulled her into his arms.

'I realise it's a cardinal sin to ruin your make-up, but there is only so much a man can stand...'

He didn't finish the sentence—couldn't, when his mouth was taking hers in a kiss that made the whole world rock on its axis. Leanne clung to him as the room began to tilt, clung even harder when it started to spin. It felt as though everything was out of control all of a sudden. She could feel her heart racing and her pulse pounding, feel her head going dizzy...

'Uncle Nick, why are you kissing that lady?'

They sprang apart when they heard a piping little voice coming from the doorway. Leanne drew in a shuddery breath as she turned to look at the little girl. It was one of Helen's daughters, and from the expression on her face she was obviously expecting Nick to answer her question.

Leanne stole a glance at him and almost burst out laughing when she saw the discomfort on his face as he tried to work out what to tell his niece. It was obviously a huge relief to him when Helen appeared to reclaim her daughter.

'Sorry about that. Melanie is at that age when she wants you to explain *everything* to her!' she said, winking at them as she shepherded the child away.

Nick groaned as they disappeared down the hall. 'That will teach me not to lock and bolt the door when there are children about. Mind you, it's more your fault than mine.'

'My fault?' Leanne said, looking at him with startled grey eyes. '*You* started kissing *me*, as I recall.'

'But only because you look so absolutely knock-down, drop-dead gorgeous that I couldn't resist.' He folded his arms and glared at her. 'How can a mere male be expected to withstand temptation?'

'Oh, I see. So what you're *really* saying is that if any half-decent female had been standing in your parents's sitting room, you wouldn't have been able to resist her?'

'No, that wasn't what I was saying, as you very well know.' He grinned at her. 'Stop tormenting me, Miss Russell. You know how I feel about you.'

'Do I?' All of a sudden the laughter seemed to drain from her and she stared at him with solemn eyes. 'I know how I feel about you, Nick. But I'm not sure if you feel the same about me.'

He closed his eyes and she saw him take a deep breath. 'It's pointless talking about it, Leanne. We both know that there's no future for us.'

'Why not? If we want to be together, we can! What's holding you back, Nick? I don't understand.'

He opened his eyes and she saw the glisten of tears on his lashes. 'All right, then, if you insist. I can never give you children, Leanne. That's why we can't let ourselves make the mistake of believing this...this attraction we feel for each other is leading anywhere.'

She was so shocked that she didn't know what to say. What did he mean, he couldn't give her children? Was he sterile or something?

She was still struggling to deal with that idea when it struck her what else he had said. Her heart seemed to jolt to a stop. Was it only *attraction* Nick felt for her and not love? Suddenly, that question seemed more important than any other, but how on earth could she ask him something like that?

Nick could tell how shocked she was. Part of him ached to explain what he'd meant, but he knew that he might be getting into even deeper waters if he did so. Would Leanne understand that it wasn't just a question of them being able to have children so long as she wasn't a carrier of Friedreich's ataxia? There was the fact that he might pass on the gene to future generations. Surely that had to be just as big a consideration?

'Leanne, I'm—'

'If you say you're sorry, Nick, I swear I won't be responsible for my actions!'

He felt his heart ache when he heard the anger in her voice because he knew that it was a mask for everything else she was feeling. Leanne was hurting—badly—and it broke his heart to know that it was all his fault.

'All right, then, I won't. But not saying it doesn't change how I feel. I wish things could have been different, Leanne, but I made up my mind a long time ago what I had to do.'

'Then there's nothing more to say on the subject, is there?' She gave him a tight smile then swiftly left the room.

Nick ached to go after her, but he made himself stay where he was until Patrick came to tell him that it was time they left. They walked through the village to the tiny parish church where he and his brothers and sisters had been baptised, and it felt as though the future had never seemed bleaker.

His children would never be baptised there. He would never experience the joy of watching them grow up. He'd thought that he'd come to terms with what he could and couldn't have, but everything had changed since he'd met Leanne. It almost broke his heart to imagine all the happiness they could have had if the situation had been different.

The service was beautiful. Leanne's eyes filled with tears as she listened to Penny and David making their vows. They were so obviously in love that their joy seemed to radiate around the church and touch the whole congregation, yet her own heart felt as cold and empty as a wasteland.

Nick didn't love her. All he felt for her was sexual attraction. It was pointless hoping that he would come to realise how important she was to him one day.

Tears poured down her cheeks and Helen, who was sitting beside her in the pew, passed her a tissue. 'Weddings always make me cry, too,' she whispered sympathetically.

Leanne smiled her thanks. There was no way she could

explain that it wasn't the service that was making her cry but the fact that her life was in tatters. Somehow she got through the rest of the day without making a spectacle of herself. She listened to the best man's speech, complimented Penny on her dress and congratulated David. She did everything that was expected of her, but she was bitterly aware that Nick was avoiding her.

Maybe he was embarrassed about what had happened and regretted having told her that he couldn't have children, but that wasn't the issue. She could have dealt with that, but she couldn't deal with the fact that he was simply *attracted* to her. By the time the band arrived and the tables were cleared away so that the dancing could begin, she'd had enough. She left the marquee and went back to the house to pack. Louise had invited her to stay overnight again but there was no way that she could bear to be around Nick, knowing how he really felt about her. She rammed her belongings into her bag and zipped it up then realised that she couldn't travel back to London on the train, dressed the way she was.

Tipping everything out onto the bed again, she found her jeans and a sweater then unzipped her dress and stepped out of it. She shoved it into the bag then spun round when the door suddenly opened and Nick appeared.

His gaze skimmed over the jumble of clothes strewn across the bed and she saw his mouth thin. 'Do I take it that you're leaving?'

'I'm going back to London.' She quickly rolled her tights down her hips, steadfastly ignoring the fact that she was standing there in her bra and panties. Nick had seen her wearing less than that the night he'd taken her back to his flat.

She threw the hose into the waste-basket, praying that he couldn't tell how that thought made her feel. It had been the most wonderful night of her entire life yet now she felt bitterly ashamed just thinking about it. Stepping into her jeans, she zipped them up then glanced at him.

'Did you want something? Or are you just here to enjoy the floor show?'

A rim of colour edged his cheekbones when he heard the bite in her voice. 'Helen said that you looked upset when you left the marquee. I came to see if you were all right.'

'How considerate of you! I'm touched.'

Her hands were trembling so much that the top snap on her jeans defeated her attempts to fasten it. In the end she left it undone and reached for her sweater, but Nick was too quick for her. He wrenched it out of her hands and tossed it onto the bed then spun her round to face him.

'Stop it, Leanne! This won't achieve anything.'

'No? I beg to differ. It makes me feel a hell of a lot better, if you really want to know!'

She pushed him away then bent to retrieve her sweater, gasping when in her haste she overbalanced. Instinctively, she grabbed hold of the nearest solid object, which just happened to be Nick, but only succeeded in pulling him over as well. They landed on the bed in a jumble of arms and legs, with him lying on top of her.

'You are one crazy lady, do you know that?'

The rumble of Nick's voice made delicious little spasms shoot through her body. His face was pressed against her bare abdomen and she could feel his lips tickling her skin when he smiled. 'There's never a dull moment when you are around, Leanne.'

'So now I'm the court jester, am I?' she said, struggling to whip up her anger again because it was safer than letting any other emotion take over.

'No, you're the most beautiful, sexy, caring and compassionate woman I've ever met. You are everything a man could want, Leanne, and more,' he said, his lips brushing her skin as he spoke so that she shivered convulsively.

'But I'm not what *you* want, am I, Nick? You made that very clear.'

It was impossible to disguise her pain and she felt him go still for a moment before he suddenly rolled over and sat up. Leanne sat up as well, feeling her heart ache when she saw the anguish in his eyes as he turned to her.

'I want you more than I have ever wanted anything in my whole life, Leanne— No. Please, don't say anything.' He pressed his fingers to her lips when she went to interrupt, then kept them there seemingly for the simple pleasure of feeling her mouth against them. And it was that which proved more than anything else could have done that he was telling her the truth.

All of a sudden her anger disappeared. The only thing she could focus on was the fact that Nick was hurting and that she wanted to comfort him. She put her arms around him and kissed him, tiny, sipping kisses which she scattered at random over his face. She could feel the tension in him, feel the way he tried to resist her, and her heart overflowed with love because she understood why.

Nick wouldn't let himself accept what she was trying to give him because he thought he had nothing to offer her in return, but he was wrong. So very wrong. He could give her another night of wonderful memories to look back on in years to come.

'Make love with me,' she murmured, pressing her lips to his cheeks, his chin, the corner of his mouth.

'I can't, Leanne! Don't you understand...?'

'Yes!' She didn't let him finish, wouldn't let him express any doubts when she was so certain about what she was doing. She needed this night, needed the memory of it to help her cope in the future.

'I know that you won't change your mind about us, Nick, but I want this. I *need* it!' Her breath caught and so did her heart because she was so afraid that she wouldn't be able to convince him. 'I think you need it, too, if you're honest with yourself.'

'Honesty is something I can't afford! I can't let myself want you, Leanne. Don't you understand? I have to protect you.'

He suddenly seemed to realise that her mouth was just a

few millimetres away from his. She heard him groan as his head turned. Their lips met and clung for the space of a single heartbeat before he broke away, and there was a note of anguish in his voice that told her how difficult he'd found it to break the contact.

'Please, sweetheart, we have to be sensible. Think how hard it will be when you go home to Australia.'

'Making love with you now won't make it any more or less difficult.' She looked into his eyes so that there could be no doubt in his mind that she was telling him the truth. 'I love you, Nick, and nothing is going to change how I feel about you. I just need this one night to look back on.'

Her voice broke and she heard him sigh raggedly. 'I should never have let this happen.'

She laughed at such a touching display of male arrogance. 'I don't think you had much control over it, I hate to tell you. Love has this nasty habit of sneaking up on people when they least expect it.'

'I suppose so.' He smiled and his eyes were full of tenderness. 'You certainly sneaked up on me, Leanne.'

She bit her lip but the question had to be asked because it was so important. 'Are you saying that it isn't just physical attraction that you feel for me?'

'Yes.'

The single word was bitten out as though it had cost him a vast amount of effort to admit it. Maybe it had, she thought as his mouth found hers, but it meant everything to her.

His mouth was hot and hungry as it plundered hers, but hers was just as hungry. Nick kissed her as though he was desperate to love her while he had the chance, and Leanne gave herself unstintingly, wanting him to know how much she loved him. Maybe it wouldn't make any difference in the end, but it seemed important that she held nothing back.

He quickly stripped off her clothes then stripped off his and locked the door before he came back to the bed. 'Let's keep everyone safely outside, shall we?'

'It might be a little more difficult to explain this to your niece,' she teased, loving the way his eyes had darkened as he looked at her.

She let her own gaze travel over the powerful planes of his chest before allowing them to follow the line of dark hair that arrowed down below his waist. She felt her body quicken, felt the hot, liquid tug of desire inside her when she saw how aroused he was.

She opened her arms to him, breathing in his scent as he came and lay beside her. She could feel the warmth of his body, hear how his breathing quickened as he skimmed a hand up over her hip and waist until he reached the swell of her breast. She knew that she was trying to store up every second so that she could build a bank of memories to draw on when he would no longer be with her.

They made love slowly yet with an intensity and passion that was unbearably moving. Their bodies fitted so perfectly together that they could have been made for each other. Nick's lips were filled with tenderness and hunger in equal measures as he kissed her, his hands so gentle as he caressed her. Leanne had a feeling that he was trying to absorb her very essence so that when they parted he would be able to conjure up her image.

She gave herself to him freely, lovingly, wanting to make this one night the most wonderful experience either of them had known—and it was. When his body finally joined with hers, she knew that she would never feel closer physically or spiritually to anyone than she felt to him. They were like two halves of one whole, so much more perfect for being together.

Nick held her in his arms after their passion was spent. They hadn't drawn the curtains and a watery moonlight lit the room. The sound of music coming from the marquee was a gentle backdrop, too faint to be intrusive. Leanne felt his fingers stroking her neck, the curve of her jaw, and sighed in contentment.

'It was like being touched with magic, wasn't it?'

'It was. If only the spell could last.'

She heard the sadness in his voice and turned towards him, not wanting anything to spoil this night. 'Don't think about that now, Nick. Don't let anything ruin this for us.'

His eyes glittered in the moonlight as he looked at her. 'You know that I would give anything for things to be different, Leanne.'

'I do.' Her voice thickened with tears because she knew he was telling her the truth. 'Are you sure we can't...?'

'No.' He kissed her hard, stopped her from saying the words he didn't want to hear, that maybe there was a way they could work things out.

Leanne's heart ached as she kissed him back, held him close, loved him. Nick had ruled out the possibility of them being together because he couldn't father a child. Even though she had always longed for a family of her own, she knew that she could have accepted it. But unless he was prepared to meet her halfway, she would never be able to convince him that they could have a future together.

The thought lent an added poignancy to their lovemaking. Tears spilled down Leanne's cheeks as Nick loved her with a tenderness that touched her soul. Neither of them slept afterwards. The hours they had together were too precious to waste on sleep.

She lay in his arms and watched dawn breaking, and her heart was heavy because the arrival of the day meant the ending of the night. She knew that it really would be the end, too, because Nick wouldn't let this happen again.

They'd had their one last night of passion and now it was over.

Nick felt a sharp pain pierce his heart as he watched the daylight creeping across the sky. Spending the night with Leanne made him ache to spend more nights with her, days, too, but it was out of the question. He wouldn't ruin her life by being selfish and taking what she was so willing to give. Maybe their love would be enough for now, but how about in the future? He didn't think he could bear it if she came to hate him for denying her the family she craved.

He tossed back the bedclothes, unable to lie there any longer and torture himself. Leanne had her eyes closed but he knew she wasn't asleep. She was trying to deal with the situation the best way she could, and it broke his heart to know that he was causing her such heartache.

He grabbed a ratty old dressing-gown from behind the door and fastened it around himself with a savage tug on the fraying cord. 'I'll make us a drink. What would you like? Tea or coffee?'

'Either. It doesn't matter.'

There was such despondency in her voice that his heart ached. He went back to the bed and gathered her into his arms, feeling her body heaving as she tried to stifle her sobs. 'Shh, sweetheart, please, don't cry. I never meant to hurt you.'

'I know you didn't.' She sniffed noisily and tried to smile. 'You did everything you could to put me off, Nick, so I don't blame you. It's my fault if I was mad enough to fall in love with you.'

Her thick, red lashes were spiky with tears, her eyelids hot and damp when he touched them with his lips. His heart spilled over with love for her, but he couldn't make the situation worse by telling her that.

'I don't know which way to take that,' he said, doing his best to inject a little levity into his voice.

He kissed her gently on the mouth then stood up because he didn't trust himself to continue being sensible if he held her any longer. Another minute and he would pour out the whole story, let her convince him that the problem *wasn't* insurmountable and that they *could* do something about it, and that was a risk he wouldn't take.

The house was very quiet as he went down to the kitchen. He filled the kettle then stood by the window and watched the grey November dawn breaking over the garden. The marquee suddenly appeared from the gloom, startling him because he'd forgotten it was there. Everything that had happened the day before was a blank. The only thing he could remember was the night.

He closed his eyes and let it all come flooding back, feeling his body quicken as he recalled how it had felt to make love to Leanne right there in the room he'd had since he was a child...

His brain snagged on that thought, although for a moment he didn't grasp its importance. Then all of a sudden his heart began to pound. Nick opened his eyes and stared out of the window at the misty November dawn while a feeling of sickness filled him.

When he'd made love to Leanne last night he hadn't taken any precautions to prevent her getting pregnant.

CHAPTER NINE

LEANNE had showered and dressed by the time Nick arrived back with two mugs of tea.

'I thought you'd got lost,' she teased, taking one of the mugs from him and sitting down on the bed. 'You've been gone ages.'

'Have I? Sorry.'

He took his tea to the window and stood there, looking out. Leanne felt a ripple of alarm run down her spine as she looked at his ramrod-straight back because it was obvious there was something troubling him.

'Is something wrong?' she asked, trying her best to hide how scared she felt all of a sudden.

'There might be.' He glanced round and she felt her nerves tighten that bit more when she saw the grim expression on his face. 'I never used any contraception last night, Leanne. Could it cause a problem?'

'No. I'm on the Pill. I decided after what happened between us a few weeks ago that it would be silly to take any risks,' she explained, then frowned. Nick had told her that he couldn't have children so why was he worried about her getting pregnant?

Unless he had lied to her?

A wave of sickness washed over her and abruptly she put down her mug. Nick was watching her and there was something about the look in his eyes that made her go cold.

'I thought you told me that you couldn't have children?' Her voice sounded strained and she saw a nerve start to tick in his jaw.

'I did.'

'Then why are you worried that I might get pregnant? I'm

sorry, Nick, but I don't understand. Exactly what is going on?'

She didn't want to believe that he had lied to her, but it was the only explanation that made any sense. Nick had made no secret of the fact that he wasn't looking for commitment so maybe he'd told her that he couldn't have children as an excuse to avoid it. How *convenient* it would be to have such a perfect reason to opt out of a relationship.

She shot to her feet, unable to sit there while such thoughts raced through her head. 'It was all a pack of lies, wasn't it? That whole story about you not being able to have children was just something you dreamt up. You're quite happy to have an affair with me, but that's as far as it goes. No wonder you kept insisting that we didn't have a future!'

'No! It isn't that simple, Leanne. You don't understand—'

'Oh, but I do!' She gave a harsh laugh because now she knew that she was right. The proof was the fact that he was trying to explain his actions rather than deny her accusation. 'You lied to me, Nick. I'm afraid it really is *that* simple!'

'That's where you're wrong, Leanne. There's nothing simple about this situation, believe me.'

There was a hollow note in his voice that brought her up short, and she frowned. It was obvious that he was upset about what she had said and yet that didn't gel with the image of a man who, apparently, would lie at will. Maybe she would come to regret this, but all of a sudden she knew that she had to make him tell her the truth.

'Then why don't you explain why you told me yesterday that you couldn't have children when it obviously isn't true? I think I have the right to know, don't you, Nick?'

Her voice broke because it was so difficult to cope with the thought that he had lied to her. She saw an expression of intense pain cross his face before he swung round and stared out of the window again. And when he spoke it was as though he had deliberately distanced himself from what was happening.

'What I told you wasn't a lie, Leanne, although, physically, I am capable of fathering a child. However, the fact is that I can never have children because I'm a carrier of Friedreich's ataxia. Bluntly, it means that any children I might have would run the risk of either contracting the disorder or being a carrier of it.'

'Friedreich's ataxia?' She sank onto the bed because her legs no longer seemed capable of holding her. 'Isn't that some kind of—of neurological disorder?'

'That's right.' He glanced round and she felt her heart ache when she saw the shuttered expression on his face. It was hard to believe that just an hour ago she'd felt closer to him than she'd felt to anyone in her whole life.

'Friedreich's ataxia is similar to multiple sclerosis in many ways. It causes problems with speech, balance and co-ordination and, although it's not considered terminal, it is progressive and often causes serious complications with the cardiac and respiratory systems.'

He took a deep breath but his voice seemed to grate as he added, 'That's what happened in Matt's case. He died of heart failure when he was twenty-six.'

'I'm so sorry. I had no idea...'

She broke off because it was pointless saying that. Nick must know that she'd had no idea why his brother had died because he hadn't told her. He would never have told her now, in fact, if she hadn't pushed him into it. It was painful to realise that he had deliberately shut her out so that it was an effort to concentrate when he carried on.

'I hope you understand now why I told you what I did, Leanne. All I can say is that I never intended to hurt you.'

'Because you never planned on getting involved with me?'

She summoned a smile but it hurt to have to face the truth. 'That's why you've always insisted that we don't have a future, isn't it, Nick?'

'Yes. I decided a long time ago that I could never risk getting involved with anyone, Leanne. It wouldn't be fair to any woman to deny her a family.'

I'm not just *any* woman, she wanted to shout, but he didn't give her the chance.

'At least we both understood the situation from the outset, even though you weren't aware of all the facts.' He shrugged. 'I'm only sorry that I upset you by not explaining everything sooner, and I'm doubly sorry for not having taken proper precautions last night. I would never have forgiven myself if I had put you at risk in any way through my own carelessness.'

'It isn't a problem,' she said hollowly, struggling to deal with how it made her feel to hear him apologise like that.

It made her wonder if last night had been as special for him as it had been for her. At the time she'd believed that their love-making had been an outpouring of their feelings for each other, but if that were the case then surely he couldn't treat her so distantly now?

'Thankfully not,' he said flatly. 'Although it doesn't make me feel any better. I should have thought about what we were doing at the time.'

'It isn't always easy to be sensible when there are emotions involved,' she suggested quietly. She held her breath, hoping—*praying*—that he would admit that he had been swept away by his feelings for her. If he did that then surely they could find a way to resolve this problem? Even though she had always longed for a family of her own, there were other options—like adoption, for instance. All it needed was for Nick to admit that he loved her.

'Emotions don't enter into it. It should never have happened, Leanne, and there's no excuse.'

There was no warmth in his voice, no trace of tenderness, nothing at all to make her believe that he really cared for her. A searing pain ran through her because she couldn't ignore the truth any longer. No matter how difficult this situation was, they could have found a solution if it was what Nick had wanted.

It was an effort to hide how much it hurt to realise that. Only pride dictated that she must never let him see how devastated she felt. She stood up, praying that she could carry this off because the last thing she wanted was to embarrass them both.

'We all do things we regret, Nick, so don't give yourself a hard time about what happened last night.' She shrugged when he looked at her sceptically. 'All right, I know it won't be easy to follow that advice, but I'm going to try to do so.'

'Meaning that you regret sleeping with me?'

There was a note in his voice that brought her eyes winging to his face, but his expression gave away nothing about his feelings. If he was upset by the idea then it certainly didn't show, she realised sickly. The thought gave her the strength to continue.

'I find you very attractive, Nick, but I realise now that I don't feel the same about you as I do about Michael. I just wish I'd found that out sooner.'

Her voice held the ring of sincerity and she saw him tense. For a moment he stared into her eyes and she had the feeling that he was trying to gauge if she was telling him the truth.

She held his gaze, praying that he couldn't tell how much it had cost her to twist the facts like that. She *didn't* feel the same about him as she did about Michael. That bit was certainly true. However, it was the interpretation that Nick would put on her words which hurt so bitterly. She loved him so much that what she had felt for Michael didn't bear comparison.

'Then all I can say is that I'm glad we've managed to sort everything out, Leanne. My main concern was that there wouldn't be any repercussions from last night.'

'Don't worry, Nick, there's no chance that I might be pregnant.' She summoned a smile but it felt as though someone had just ripped open her heart. 'The last thing I want is to go home with that kind of a memento from my visit.'

'No. I don't suppose Michael would appreciate it either.'

He swung round before she could answer and went to the door then glanced back. 'I'm driving Gareth back to London after breakfast if you want a lift. He's flying back to New York and needs to be at the airport by eleven.'

'No. It's fine. Thank you.' She managed to hold her smile. 'I'll probably spend the day here and do some sightseeing. I don't expect I'll have a chance to visit the area again so I may as well make the most of it.'

'Fine. I'm sure Mum will be pleased to have you stay a while longer.' He gave her a quick, almost dismissive smile then left the room. Leanne heard his footsteps going down the stairs and sank onto the bed as her legs suddenly gave way. She had no intention of staying after he left. It had been an excuse to save having to travel back to London with him. She didn't think she could bear being near him after what had happened.

She closed her eyes, struggling to come to terms with what had happened. Maybe she should have been more upset about him being a carrier of Friedreich's ataxia but she couldn't seem to get past the thought that he didn't love her. Everything else seemed to come second to that.

Nick didn't love her. When she went home to Australia he wouldn't give her another thought.

She made herself recite the facts in the hope that it would help if she got used to the idea. It didn't work.

She opened her eyes and stared at her reflection in the mirror on the dressing table. It made no difference how Nick felt about her because she still loved him. She always would.

The journey back to London was a nightmare. Nick couldn't stop thinking about what Leanne had told him. If she'd physically ripped out his heart it couldn't have hurt any more than hearing her say that she didn't love him.

He clashed the gears, ignoring the startled look Gareth shot him. Fortunately, Gareth must have decided not to comment but it wouldn't have mattered if he had. Nothing mattered now that Leanne had told him that it was Michael she loved and not him!

Pain tore through him again and he stifled a groan. They

were approaching Heathrow Airport now and the traffic was getting heavier. Nick made himself concentrate as he drove Gareth to his terminal then returned the car to the rental agency. He handed over the keys and signed the paperwork without even bothering to check if the details were correct.

What did it matter if they lumped extra charges on the bill? What did *anything* matter any more?

In his heart he knew that he should be berating himself for the mistake he had made the previous night by putting Leanne at risk. He had always been so careful in the past but last night he'd been swept away by his feelings for her. He loved her *so much* and would have given anything in the world to have been able to keep her in his life, but what was the point of even thinking about that now?

A bitter laugh welled into his throat as he thought about all the heart-searching he had done recently. He had been so worried about doing the right thing, so afraid that he would ruin Leanne's life, when the truth was that it made no difference what *he* did. It was Michael she wanted, Michael she loved, Michael who would be the father of her children, not him.

'There's a patient in Reception I think you should see, Dr Slater.'

It was midway through Monday morning, the worst morning of her entire life. Leanne had been dreading seeing Nick when she'd come to work that day, and it had been every bit as bad as she'd feared. True, he had treated her with the utmost politeness but the fact that he could be so *distant* with her hurt unbearably. Now, as he looked up, she had to steel herself when she saw the total absence of warmth in his eyes.

'Is there a problem?'

'I think so.' It was an effort to keep her tone as impersonal as his had been. 'The patient is complaining of severe pain in her right upper abdomen. She's also been vomiting through the night.'

'I'll take a look at her, then.'

He got up from the desk and Leanne hastily made her way out of the door. She didn't look at him as she led the way to the treatment room but she was aware of him following her along the corridor. She reached for the doorhandle then jumped when Nick reached for it as well and their hands touched. She couldn't stop herself looking at him then and felt her heart ache when she saw the regret in his eyes.

'I'm sorry, Leanne. This has all turned into rather a mess, hasn't it? That's the last thing I wanted to happen, too.'

'Don't worry about it.'

She went to open the door but he forestalled and she shivered when she felt his fingers tighten around hers as he stopped her turning the handle.

'I can't help but worry,' he said roughly, and she was shocked by the emotion she could hear in his voice all of a sudden. Her eyes flew to his face again and she felt her heart race when she saw how anguished he looked.

Was it possible that Nick cared because she was upset? she wondered, before the truth hit her. The only thing Nick cared about was making sure there were no repercussions from their night of passion.

'I already told you there's no danger of me being pregnant.' She smiled tightly at him. 'Don't worry, Nick. There really is no need to give it another thought.'

'Dammit, Leanne, I—'

'We have a patient waiting, Dr Slater.'

She didn't let him finish because she couldn't bear to hear what he had to say. It wouldn't help to hear him repeat that he had never intended this to happen. Maybe Nick had a valid reason for believing that he should avoid commitment, but if he'd *cared* about her, they could have worked through this problem.

It was a sobering thought, but Leanne did her best not to think about it as she introduced him to the patient. Margaret Lomas was an elegantly dressed woman in her fifties, an American who was visiting England with her husband to celebrate their thirtieth wedding anniversary. Even though she was in a lot of pain, she was wearing full make-up. However, no amount of cosmetics could disguise the unhealthy yellow tinge to her skin.

'I'm Nick Slater, acting head of the clinic.' Nick quickly introduced himself, then smiled reassuringly. 'Nurse tells me that you're in a lot of pain, Mrs Lomas, so would you mind if I examine you?'

'Please, do, Doctor.' Margaret Lomas grimaced. 'I've never felt pain like it before. I didn't sleep a wink last night because I was in such agony.'

'Then let's not waste any time finding out what's wrong with you.' Nick carefully examined her, paying particular attention to the area where the pain was at its worst. He turned to Leanne when he had finished and she had to steel herself not to show how much it hurt to have him look at her with such a lack of emotion.

'I'd like a white blood cell count done so will you take a blood sample and get it to the lab, please?'

'Of course, sir.'

She turned away, glad to have an excuse not to look at him. Taking a fresh syringe from the drawer, she placed it in a kidney dish then took a pair of latex gloves from the box on the shelf. She bit her lip when she discovered that she was trembling so hard that it was impossible to get her hands into the gloves. How on earth could she take blood from a patient in this state?

She dropped the gloves onto the desk and made for the door, ignoring the questioning look Nick shot at her. Kim Chang was manning Reception so she asked her if she would mind helping Nick because she wasn't feeling well.

It wasn't a lie because she felt sick and shaken, as though her whole world was caving in on top of her. As she sat down behind the desk, Leanne realised that working at the clinic was going to be impossible from now on. She couldn't expect the rest of the staff to keep covering for her, neither could she avoid working with Nick. It meant there was only one option open to her.

She would have to hand in her notice and leave. And if she did that, she may as well go home to Australia because there was nothing to keep her in England. She had found no trace of her mother and doubted if she ever would now that she'd exhausted all her leads. At any rate, it no longer seemed important that she should find her. The only thing that mattered now was that Nick didn't love her.

Tears filled her eyes and she blinked them away because there was no point crying when it wouldn't change anything.

'I have the results of those blood tests you wanted, Dr Slater.'

Nick looked round as Kim Chang came into the room with a slip of paper. He took it from her with a murmur of thanks, but it was hard to disguise his concern when he had been hoping that Leanne would come back. Kim had whispered to him that Leanne wasn't feeling well when she'd arrived to help him, but that had been almost an hour ago. Surely she should be feeling better by now?

His heart kicked in an extra couple of beats at the thought that she might be ill. It was all he could do not to rush off to find her, but he had a duty to his patient first. He would have to wait until he'd sorted out this problem before he could check on Leanne.

'So are you any the closer to knowing what's wrong with my wife, Doctor?'

He looked up when Harold Lomas, Margaret's husband, drew his attention to the fact that he had been standing there, staring at the lab results. From the worried expression on the man's face he was obviously fearing the worst, so Nick hurried to reassure him.

'This confirms my suspicions that your wife is probably suffering from gallstones, Mr Lomas. Her white cell count is higher than it should be, and allied to her other symptoms—the pain in the upper right quarter of her abdomen, the nausea and jaundice—it's a strong indication that gallstones are the problem, probably lodged in one of the bile ducts.'

'Gallstones!' Margaret clutched her husband's hand. 'That means I'll need an operation!'

'There, there, honey. Don't you fret.' Harold patted her hand. He sighed as he looked at Nick. 'Does it mean an operation, Dr Slater?'

Nick perched on the end of the desk, hoping that his impatience to get this over with didn't show. It wasn't their fault that he had made such a mess of everything.

'Let's take things a step at a time, shall we? First of all we need to do something to alleviate your discomfort, Mrs Lomas. Biliary colic is best treated with bed rest and injections of analgesic so I'll refer you to hospital. The doctors there will deal with the pain and arrange for further tests to be carried out, probably an ultrasound scan to determine how big the stones are and exactly where they are lodged in your system.'

'Oh, I don't think I want to go to a hospital over here!'

Margaret Lomas was becoming very agitated. Nick sighed because he could tell that it was going to take some time to calm her down. He had never resented spending time with a patient before but he resented it now when Leanne needed him...

Why should he imagine that she needed him? a small voice inside his head whispered. If she *needed* anyone, surely it was Michael?

It was hard to contain the pain that thought caused him. He took a deep breath but it did little to ease his anguish at the thought of Leanne and the other man.

'Please, don't upset yourself, Mrs Lomas. I doubt if they will keep you in more than a few days. Once they have established the size and extent of the gallstones, they will have a better idea of the kind of treatment you'll require.'

'What sort of treatment, Dr Slater?' Harold interjected.

'That will be up to the consultant to decide. The most

common method is surgical removal of the stones. Nowadays it's usually done by keyhole surgery, which means that the recovery time afterwards is much shorter than it used to be.

'However, if the stones are small enough they can be treated with ultrasound shock waves—the stones are shattered by being bombarded with sound waves and pass out of the body naturally. Or, in some cases, drugs are used to dissolve them.'

'I see.' Harold squeezed his wife's hand. 'It doesn't sound too bad, honey.'

'Maybe not to you, but it isn't *you* who has to put up with it,' she retorted.

Harold winked at Nick. 'Why do I have a feeling that I'm going to end up taking the blame for this, along with all the other things I've done wrong in the past thirty years? Married life sure ain't no picnic—not that I would want to change a thing,' he added hastily when Margaret glared at him.

Nick laughed but it was hard to hide his anguish. He would never have the chance to find out what married life was like, would he?

He quickly excused himself, but instead of going straight to his office to phone the hospital he went to Reception. Leanne was manning the desk and she looked round when she heard him coming along the corridor. Nick felt his insides twist with agony when he saw her look away. It was obvious that she couldn't bear to look at him after what had happened on Saturday night and it hurt to know how bitterly she regretted it.

'Kim said that you weren't feeling well,' he said, doing his best not to let his feelings show.

'I'm fine.' She picked up an envelope from the desk and held it out to him. 'I'm not sure if I should give this to you or to Dennis.'

'What is it?' he asked, automatically taking it from her.

'My letter of resignation.' She shrugged when he looked

at her in dismay. 'I think it's better if I leave, Nick. Working together would be far too stressful after...'

She trailed off, either unable or unwilling to finish the sentence. There was a buzzing sound in Nick's ears, a heaviness in his chest, but he forced himself to ignore them. 'Are you sure about this, Leanne?'

'Quite sure. I'm going back to Australia as soon as I can book myself onto a flight.'

'Do you really think that's the right thing to do?' he demanded, his heart ricocheting around his ribs faster than a speeding bullet. The thought of her leaving was bad enough, but knowing that she was going back to Australia was even worse.

He dredged his mind for a way to persuade her to stay. Maybe it was pointless, drawing out the agony, but he couldn't bear to think of her being on the other side of the world, so far away.

'What about finding your mother? If you go back home, you might never get another chance to trace her.'

'I've more or less given up any hope of finding her. There's no point staying any longer, Nick. There's nothing to stay for.'

There's me! he wanted to shout, but what was the point when she'd told him that she didn't love him?

He turned away, knowing that he couldn't trust himself not to say something he might regret. It wouldn't be fair to make her feel awful because Leanne didn't love him.

He went back to his office and picked up the phone but he couldn't see the numbers he needed to dial for the tears that filled his eyes. Leanne was going home and he would never see her again. He didn't know how he was going to bear being apart from her.

The morning finally ended and it was time for her to leave. Leanne collected her coat from the staffroom and hurried through the clinic. She was just about to enter Reception when Dennis McNally accosted her and she was forced to stop.

'Nick's just given me your letter of resignation, Leanne. I'm really sorry to hear that you'll be leaving us. It's not something that has happened here that has caused you to hand in your notice, I hope?'

She shook her head, wanting only to make her escape before Nick appeared. She had sent a patient through to him a short time before and it wouldn't be long before he was free. 'No, I just decided that I wanted to go home, that's all.'

'Homesick, are you?' Dennis smiled sympathetically. 'Obviously, you're not like the rest of the staff who work here, then.'

'Sorry?' she murmured distractedly, glancing behind her when she heard a door opening. She felt her heart surge when she saw Nick ushering out his patient and hurriedly turned back to Dennis again.

'I meant that you haven't got itchy feet. You're more a homebody.' Dennis glanced at Nick as he passed them and winked at her. 'Unlike some I could mention.'

'Yes.' She pasted a smile to her mouth but it was an effort not to show how much that comment had upset her. Nick had chosen the kind of life he led because of what had happened to his brother. All of a sudden it was crystal clear. He was afraid to put down roots in case he met a woman and fell in love with her.

It hurt to know how lonely his life really was, but there was nothing she could do about it. If Nick had fallen in love with her, she would have found a way to convince him that he need never be lonely again. But Nick didn't love her and there was nothing at all that she could do.

She quickly excused herself before Dennis realised she was upset. Nick was nowhere in sight when she went through Reception and she breathed a sigh of relief. It was going to be difficult to avoid him while she worked out her notice, but she would just have to do the best she could to get through the coming days.

The thought had barely crossed her mind when she spotted him crossing the concourse below. Even though the station was packed with commuters, she had no problem picking him out. She felt her eyes well with tears as she realised that she could have picked him out of any crowd in any city in the world because he was so special to her.

Leanne quickly made her way down the steps, meaning to go straight to the travel bureau to book her flight home. She had bought an open-return ticket and was hoping there wouldn't be a problem getting a seat. Now that she had made up her mind to leave, she didn't want any delays.

She hurried towards the main exit then paused when she saw a familiar figure sitting on the floor by the tobacconist's kiosk and realised that it was the pregnant teenager, Amy. She went over to speak to her and realised immediately there was something seriously wrong with the girl.

'What's the matter?' she asked, crouching beside her.

'I've got these terrible pains...' Amy groaned, beads of sweat standing out on her forehead as she clutched her stomach.

Leanne put her hand on the girl's swollen belly and frowned. 'When did they start?'

'About an hour ago. I had terrible backache last night and thought I must have caught a chill...' Amy moaned as the pain began once more.

Leanne stood up and looked around, wondering where the nearest telephone was situated. There was no doubt in her mind that Amy was in labour and she desperately needed to call an ambulance to take her to a hospital.

'Don't leave me!' The girl clutched at Leanne's coat. 'Please. I'm really scared!'

'Shh, it's all right, love. I'm not going to leave you for very long.' She crouched down again and patted the teenager's hand. 'You're in labour, Amy, and I need to get you to a hospital. I'll have to call an ambulance.'

'In labour? But I can't be. I'm only eight months pregnant and the baby shouldn't be born for *ages* yet!'

The girl's distress was pitiful to see. Leanne put her arms around her and hugged her. 'It will be all right, love. Honestly, it will. Babies survive when they're born much earlier than this.'

She looked round when she heard hurried footsteps approaching, and felt her heart lift with relief when she saw Nick heading towards them. What had happened between them in the past forty-eight hours suddenly seemed irrelevant as she realised how glad she was to see him.

'What's happened?' he demanded, crouching beside them. His eyebrows drew together in concern when he heard Amy moan as another contraction began. 'She's in labour? Have you called an ambulance?'

'I was just going to do so, but she didn't want me to leave her,' Leanne explained, unable to hide her relief at seeing him.

'I see.' He glanced at her and she felt her head whirl when she caught a glimpse of something in his eyes that she'd never expected to see again. To have Nick looking at her with such tenderness confused her totally. If he felt nothing for her, why was he looking at her that way?

'You stay here with her, Leanne, while I phone for an ambulance. I'll be as quick as I can.'

It was too much of an effort to respond so she merely nodded as he got up and ran across the concourse to the public phone boxes. Amy was becoming very distressed as the contractions got stronger so Leanne concentrated all her energies on helping her. However, a tiny part of her brain was struggling to understand what was happening.

If Nick cared about her, why was he so determined to push her out of his life?

CHAPTER TEN

QUITE a crowd had gathered by the time Nick arrived back from phoning for the ambulance. He pushed his way through the onlookers and crouched down beside Leanne.

'Ambulance should be here in roughly ten minutes,' he told her, seeing the concern in her beautiful grey eyes when she looked up.

'It might be too late by then. Everything seems to have speeded up and her contractions are coming just minutes apart now.'

She had barely finished speaking when Amy gave a keening wail. Nick glanced round, realising that he needed to find somewhere private where he could examine the girl. His gaze alighted on a figure standing at the back of the crowd, and he stood up.

'Where are you going?' Leanne demanded.

'Don't worry, I'm not deserting you.'

He pointed towards the woman at the back of the crowd, trying to stop his pulse from racing when he saw the relief in her eyes. The thought that she was glad to have him there made him want to leap up and down before it struck him that her desire for his company wasn't personal but stemmed from her concern for Amy. It was an effort to hide how deflated that thought made him feel.

'If I'm not mistaken, that woman is in charge of the tobacconist's kiosk. I'm going to see if she'll let us take Amy in there while we examine her.'

'Good idea!' she exclaimed, smiling up at him.

Nick felt his heart kick into overdrive again and hastily turned away, not sure that he could trust himself not to make a fool of himself. Leanne didn't love him, she loved

155

Michael, he told himself as he pushed his way through the crowd, but the words seemed to fall on deaf ears. The long and the short of it was that he didn't want to think about her loving anyone but him.

It took a bit of persuasion, but finally the assistant agreed to let them use the kiosk. Nick went back and helped Amy to her feet, wishing that he could have taken her back to the clinic where they would have had everything they needed to hand. However, he quailed at the thought of carrying the girl across the station in her present state. The baby could arrive at any minute and he didn't relish the idea of delivering it in the middle of the concourse. At least they would have some privacy in the kiosk.

'Help me get her down on the floor,' he instructed Leanne, who had followed with Amy's belongings.

She dropped the carrier bags onto the counter then went to help him, and between them they made the teenager comfortable. Nick turned to the assistant who had followed them into the kiosk.

'We work at HealthFirst—the clinic on the gallery—so would you mind running over there and telling the nurse on duty in Reception what has happened? My name is Nick Slater, and if you could tell her that I need some sheets and towels, and anything else she can think of that might be useful, I'd be grateful.'

The woman nodded before she rushed out of the door. Leanne got up and closed it behind her, turning the sign over to indicate that the kiosk was no longer open for business. Taking off her coat, she used it to make a pillow for Amy's head then knelt beside her and held her hand.

Nick felt his insides spasm with tenderness when he saw how gently she treated the terrified teenager. Leanne was so kind and caring, so concerned about other people. It made him feel even worse about what had happened on Sunday morning.

All of a sudden he knew that they needed to talk about what had gone on. He couldn't bear to think that she would return home, feeling guilty about what they'd done. If he made her understand that they had both been carried away by their feelings and that she shouldn't blame herself, it might help. If it also meant him confessing how he really felt about her then so be it. As long as Leanne didn't look back on the time they had spent together and feel ashamed, that would be compensation enough.

There was no time to do anything about it right then with Amy to attend to. Nick quickly examined the girl and realised that Leanne had been right about the baby's imminent arrival. The girl's cervix was fully dilated and he could see the baby's head crowning.

'We're going to have to do the best we can until the ambulance gets here, but this isn't going to be easy for her,' he told Leanne as he drew her aside. 'I need you to keep Amy as calm as possible.'

'Fine.' She fixed a smile to her mouth before she went back and knelt beside the girl. Nick saw her squeeze the teenager's hand and felt a wave of love wash over him that was so intense that it almost brought him to his knees. It was only the arrival of the kiosk assistant with a bundle of sheets and towels that kept him going, in fact.

Nick thanked the woman then ushered her outside while Leanne made a makeshift bed out of some of the sheets for the baby to be delivered on. Amy's contractions were getting stronger and he knew that he needed to slow things down to lessen the risk to the infant.

'Try not to push. Next time you feel a contraction begin, I want you to pant like this.'

He quickly demonstrated what he wanted her to do, thinking wistfully how much easier it would have been if the girl had attended antenatal classes. However, to give Amy her due, she did her best to follow his instructions even though he could tell how scared she was.

Leanne was talking to her in a low voice, calming and encouraging her as the waves of pain ebbed and flowed. She exuded such a feeling of confidence that he knew it was mainly due to her being there that Amy was coping so well.

He turned his attention to doing his bit, supporting the baby's head as it started to emerge and tearing away the thin membrane that covered its face. He hurriedly eased the cord over its head when he discovered that it was looped around the child's neck and in danger of strangling it. One shoulder slid out and he gently raised the infant's head a fraction so that the other shoulder would follow. Then, with a little rush, the rest of its body emerged.

It was a little boy, rather small but perfectly formed. Nick knew that their biggest problem was making sure that the infant started breathing. He quickly ran the tip of his finger around the child's mouth to clear away any mucus then tipped him upside down so that any fluid he might have swallowed during the delivery would drain from his lungs.

'How is he?' Leanne asked worriedly.

'He'll be fine once I get him breathing,' he replied, hoping that he wasn't being overly confident. It had been some time since he'd delivered a baby, and then it had been in the comfort and security of a well-equipped maternity unit. However, he didn't intend to fail, having got this far.

He gently tapped the soles of the baby's feet to encourage it to cry, and grinned when it let out a shrill wail of displeasure. 'Yes!'

His cry of delight was echoed by the pleasure in Leanne's eyes and he felt his heart lift with joy. Maybe he was being ridiculously sentimental but it seemed right that they should share this special moment. Nothing could be more wonderful than watching a new life coming into the world.

Unless it was watching their own child being born, of course.

The thought was so painful that his mind seemed to go numb. Several seconds must have elapsed before he realised that Leanne had spoken to him.

'I'm sorry, what was that?' he said, trying his best to hide how he felt. However, the moment he heard the concern in her voice he knew that he hadn't fooled her.

'I asked if everything was all right,' she said, her eyes searching his face.

'If you mean with the baby, yes, he appears to be fine,' he said shortly, turning away to attend to the task of cutting the cord. He wrapped the baby in a towel and handed him to Leanne then looked round when the door opened and a paramedic appeared.

'Looks like reinforcements have arrived,' he said, making a determined effort to behave as though everything was fine, although it was a long way from being that. The thought that he would never see his own child coming into the world almost broke his heart. It didn't seem fair that he would be denied the joy of being a parent, but what could he do? Could he really live with the thought that he might pass on the defective gene to his children and grandchildren?

He tried not to think about it as they handed Amy over to the ambulance crew. The girl was exhausted by her ordeal but she smiled at them as the paramedics loaded her onto a stretcher and handed her baby son to her.

'Thank you both.' She dropped a kiss on the baby's head and there were tears in her eyes when she looked up. 'I don't know what would have happened if you hadn't been here.'

'It was our pleasure.' Leanne bent and hugged her. 'You just take care of yourself and that beautiful little boy. Maybe I can visit you both in hospital?'

'I'd like that.' Amy grimaced. 'I might even phone my mum and tell her what's happened. What do you think?'

'I think it's a wonderful idea,' Leanne said immediately. 'I'm sure she'll be thrilled to hear from you. She must have been very worried about you these past months.'

'I suppose so,' Amy agreed, before the ambulance crew whisked her away.

Nick took a deep breath as he watched the convoy disappearing out of the doors. It was a relief to know that the pair would soon be receiving the care they needed. He looked round when he heard Leanne blowing her nose, and frowned when he realised that she was crying.

'Hey, come on. I know the baby is rather small but a few days in the special care baby unit and he'll be fine.'

'I know he will. It's just that I can't help wondering what happened when my mother had me. I only hope there was someone there to help her.'

She blew her nose again but more tears were already welling from her eyes. It seemed like the most natural thing in the world when he took her in his arms. He ran his hand over her hair, feeling her slender body heaving with sobs. It hurt so much to witness her distress and he wasn't sure what to do about it...

Afterwards, he wasn't sure what had made him kiss her. He certainly hadn't been planning on doing so after what had happened. But holding Leanne in his arms and knowing how unhappy she was feeling was more than he could bear.

Her lips were soft and damp from her tears. Nick could taste the salt on them and his heart overflowed with tenderness. He drew her closer, hoping that she could tell how much he loved her, hoping it would help.

A searing pain ran through him as he realised how foolish that was. What difference did it make to her how *he* felt? It was Michael she loved, Michael's arms she wanted to feel around her, Michael's kisses she longed for. And yet when he let her go there was nothing about her expression that hinted that she had found his kiss distasteful.

Nick felt his insides spasm with shock when he saw the yearning in her eyes. Why was she looking at *him* like that when it was Michael she wanted? His heart had already started to race even before she spoke, and it seemed to be aiming for a new world record when he heard the urgency in her voice.

'I thought I understood what was going on, Nick, but now I'm confused. Why did you kiss me like that if you don't care for me?'

* * *

Leanne held her breath as she waited for Nick to answer. Maybe it was foolish to ask that question, but she needed to hear the answer. She had to find out how he really felt about her.

'Of course, I care about you, Leanne! You know I do.'

She flinched when she heard the pain in his voice. She didn't want to upset him but she had to make him explain. 'I don't know anything of the sort, not after what happened on Sunday—'

She broke off as a crowd of football supporters came rushing into the station. Nick quickly steered her out of their way, waiting until they had reached a relatively quiet spot before he spoke, and there was a new urgency in his voice that made her tremble.

'We can't talk here, Leanne. Quite apart from the fact that it's too damned noisy, I need to get back to work. Can we meet tonight and try to sort this out?'

'If you're sure that's what you want—' she began.

'I am!' He took hold of her hands and held them tightly. 'I can't bear the thought of you hating me because of what has happened.'

'I could never hate you, Nick,' she whispered, unable to lie.

She heard him take a deep breath but his voice seemed to grate when he continued. 'You have no idea how good it is to hear you say that. So can I come to your flat tonight after work?'

'Yes. I'd like that, Nick. I...I don't want there to be any bad feelings between us when I go home to Australia.'

She saw an expression of pain cross his face, but she knew it would be silly to assume there would be a happy ending from this. Nick had made his views on commitment perfectly clear and there was no reason to think that he'd changed his mind.

'I'll see you around six then. OK?' He gave her fingers a final squeeze and let her go.

'OK,' she repeated obediently.

She watched him walking across the concourse then turned and headed for the door. There was a travel agent's shop on the corner of the road and she made straight for it. There was a seat available on a flight leaving London that Friday, so she asked the clerk to reserve it for her then went home and spent the rest of the day praying that she wouldn't have to get on the plane.

If Nick would only tell her tonight that he loved her, she would find a way to convince him that they could have a future despite all the obstacles in their path.

The afternoon seemed to drag. Nick found himself constantly watching the clock. The clinic was quiet for once, which just seemed to make the time pass even more slowly, although, typically, they had a rush just before six o'clock when he was due to leave.

He saw a couple of patients, thanking his lucky stars that there was nothing seriously wrong with them, then left the clinic shortly before seven. The evening rush hour was tailing off so he managed to catch the tube to Euston without any difficulty.

Leanne lived just a short walk away from the station so he went straight to her flat, feeling his nerves humming with tension when he rang her bell. He had tried to work out what to say to her but it was hard to know the best way to handle this meeting. Maybe it would help if he simply stuck to his main objective of making her feel better about what had happened.

Telling her that he loved her was probably the wrong thing to do when he didn't want to put any more pressure on her. He had to remember that, no matter what had happened that afternoon, it was Michael she really loved.

She came to the door to let him in and Nick felt his heart ache when he saw the strain on her face. It was obvious how difficult this was for her and he wished with all his heart that he'd put a stop to what had been happening sooner. If he'd been strong enough to walk away when he'd realised how deep his feelings for her were, she wouldn't be going through this torment now.

'Please, sit down.' She led the way into her flat, grimacing as she ushered him towards the single armchair. 'It's not very comfortable, I'm afraid. Most of the springs seem to be broken.'

'Don't worry.' Nick sat down and looked around the cramped little room. 'Not exactly the lap of luxury, is it?'

'It certainly isn't.' She gave him a quick smile then went to the tiny tabletop refrigerator and took out a bottle of white wine. 'Do you fancy a glass?'

'Please.' He took the bottle from her while she found some glasses in the cupboard, smiling when he saw from the label that it was an Australian brand. 'Being patriotic, I see.'

'More a case of watching my budget.' She flicked him another smile as she came back with the glasses and sat on the bed. 'One thing I won't miss when I return home is the cost of living in London. It's horrendously expensive here.'

'I can't disagree with you there.'

He returned her smile but he was aware that it hadn't been a passing comment. Leanne wanted him to know that, no matter what happened that night, she was going home. Maybe she thought it would make it easier for him, but it made him feel worse to know that very soon she would be living on the other side of the world.

It was an effort to hide how depressed he felt as he accepted a glass of the wine. She poured a glass for herself then looked up. Nick felt his heart lurch when he saw how nervous she looked.

'I'm not really sure where we start, Nick. On Sunday you told me that your brother died because he had Friedreich's ataxia. Am I right to think that everything hinges on that?'

'Yes.' He took a sip of his wine but his hands were trembling so hard that he had to put down the glass. 'Matt's illness had an effect on the whole family, but I suppose I was the most badly affected by it.'

'Can you explain a bit more about the disorder?' she put in quietly. 'I don't know very much about it, you see.'

'Not many people do.' He summoned a smile. 'Basically, it's an inherited genetic disorder which is caused by an abnormality in a single gene. Unless a person inherits a double dose of the defective gene, they don't contract the disorder, although they can be a carrier, which, unfortunately, I am.'

'What about your brother and sisters—are they carriers as well?'

'No.' He stared at the floor, hoping that he could contain the rush of emotions he felt. He rarely spoke about those dark days after Matt had been diagnosed with the disorder, but Leanne deserved to hear the full story.

'Mum and Dad were stunned when they found out what was wrong with Matt because they'd had no idea they were both carriers of Friedreich's. We all had to go for tests, but it turned out that Patrick, Helen and Penny are completely unaffected by it. However, the tests showed that I'm a carrier, like my parents.'

'So you won't suffer from Friedreich's ataxia, but you could pass it on to your own children?' she clarified. 'And that means that if you had a child with a woman who is also a carrier then there's a chance that it could contract the disorder like your brother did?'

'That's right. It's a bit like a lottery.' He shrugged. 'Each child of parents who both carry the defective gene has a one in four chance of developing Friedreich's.'

'I see. But if one of the parents *isn't* a carrier, there's no risk at all to the child?'

'There's no risk of the child developing the disorder, but he or she could still be a carrier of it,' he explained patiently. 'They could pass on the gene so that at some point a child from a future generation could be born with the disorder.'

'And that's why you decided never to have children, not just because of the risk to your own children but because of what might happen to future generations of your family? Is that it, Nick?'

'Exactly. I couldn't bear to imagine a child being born who would suffer the way Matt did,' he said flatly.

'But who's to say they won't find a cure for it at some point?' She bent forward and he could see the urgency in her eyes. 'You know as well as I do what massive advances have been made in gene therapy in the past few years. One day the scientists might come up with a way to eradicate the defective gene.'

'Maybe, but there's no guarantee they will find a cure, Leanne. It certainly isn't something I can bank on happening.'

'Don't you think you're being too hard on yourself?' she said quietly, and he could hear the ache in her voice. 'Hundreds of people are carriers of defective genes and never even know it.'

'But that's the whole point. I *do* know!'

He got up and paced across the room then turned to face her. 'How can I take the risk of having children when I know what might happen, Leanne? I saw how Matt suffered and I couldn't bear to go through something like that again!'

'Don't, Nick! Please, don't upset yourself. I didn't mean to rake up a whole lot of painful memories,' she said beseechingly.

'I know, and it isn't your fault, sweetheart.' He took a deep breath. 'It's just so hard to talk about Matt. I keep remembering all the plans we made when we were kids, and how he never got to live long enough to see any of them come true.'

'Did you go for counselling after he died?' She sighed when he shook his head. 'You should have done, Nick. People need help to work through this kind of a problem.'

'I didn't see any point discussing it. It certainly wouldn't have changed anything,' he said firmly, even though he couldn't help wondering if she might be right.

His parents had tried to persuade him to see a counsellor, but he'd refused, mainly because he'd found it too difficult to talk about his feelings at the time. Would he have been able to come to terms with what had happened if he had sought help? he wondered.

It was a troubling thought but he refused to think about it right then. He was more concerned about how Leanne felt at that moment. He looked up when she sighed and felt his stomach tighten when he saw the way she was looking at him so intently.

'So, basically, what you're saying, Nick, is that you've made up your mind about never having children and that you won't change it?'

'That's right,' he agreed, wishing he knew where this was leading.

'And because you've decided not to have children, you think it would be best not to get involved in a long-term relationship?'

'Yes.' His tone was clipped because it was difficult to speak when Leanne was weighing up every word he said.

'And what if I told you that it didn't matter if we couldn't have children, that so long as I had you I would be happy? Would you change your mind about us, Nick? Or wouldn't it make a scrap of difference?'

CHAPTER ELEVEN

LEANNE could feel her heart racing as she waited to hear what Nick would say. Maybe it was wrong to have put him on the spot like that, but she had done it with the very best of intentions. If Nick would only accept that she meant what she had said, they could work this out.

'I can't see any point answering questions like that,' he began, but she didn't let him finish.

'Of course there's a point! I'm telling you that it makes no difference to me if you can't have children, Nick. So long as I have you, I can deal with everything else!'

'No.' He'd started shaking his head before she had finished speaking. 'I don't want to hear this, Leanne. I know you're only trying to be kind—'

'Kind?' She gave a harsh little laugh. 'I'm not being *kind*, Nick. I'm desperate! Desperate to convince you that you're making a mistake by cutting me out of your life because of some sort of...of *noble* desire not to hurt me!'

'And it wouldn't hurt you if you never had a family? Come on, Leanne, be honest with yourself and with me. You told me that you'd always dreamed of having children and now you're claiming that it doesn't matter if you never have any?' He laughed scornfully but beneath the scorn she could hear the pain that laced his voice, and her heart ached because of what he must be going through.

'No, I'm not saying that. Of course it matters, but it matters more that we can't be together.' She took a quick step towards him, praying that she would be able to convince him that she was telling the truth.

'I love you, Nick, and there's nothing I would like more than to have your child. But if it isn't possible, I accept that.

What I can't accept is that you're pushing me away when there's no reason to do so.'

'Maybe you believe what you're saying at this precise moment, Leanne, but it's very easy to get carried away by your feelings.'

He shrugged when she looked at him in disbelief. 'I know how kind and caring you are. And I know how it must have upset you to hear about Matt's and my own situation, but it would be wrong to misinterpret feelings of pity for love.'

'Pity? Do you really believe that's all I feel for you, Nick?' She was so hurt that it was hard to speak, even more difficult when she saw the shuttered expression on his face. He didn't want to listen to what she had to say and certainly didn't want to have to believe her.

'I think it's a fairly safe assumption. You told me yourself that you don't feel the same about me as you do about Michael.'

He shook his head when she went to interrupt. 'No. Please, don't make this any more difficult than it is. My mind is made up, Leanne, and one day you'll thank me for stopping you from making such a dreadful mistake. When you hold your first child in your arms, you'll know that I was right.'

His voice broke and he turned away, but not before she'd seen the tears in his eyes. Without stopping to think about what she was doing, she put her arms around him and hugged him.

'It doesn't have to end this way, Nick,' she whispered, holding him close. If only she could *make* him believe that she knew she was right, they could have a future. Surely Nick must feel *something* for her if he was so concerned about hurting her?

'We can make this work, I know we can…'

'And to make it work you'll have to give up all your dreams.' He turned to face her, drawing her into his arms and holding her so tightly that she could feel the heavy thudding of his heart against her breast. 'I can't do that, Leanne.

I know it would be wrong, even though I shall always cherish the thought that you were prepared to sacrifice so much for me.'

'It wouldn't be a sacrifice! How could it be that when it would mean us being together?' she implored him.

'And you can swear with your hand on your heart that you won't come to regret giving up your plans to have a family? That you won't come to hate me for destroying your dreams?'

'Yes! I *can* swear that neither of those things will ever happen.' Her voice broke but she struggled on, desperate to convince him that she meant every word. 'I could never hate you, Nick. Never!'

'Never is a long time, sweetheart, and nobody can promise that they'll feel the same in five, ten or even fifteen years.'

He bent and kissed her gently on the mouth. Leanne felt tears fill her eyes because she knew that it was a farewell kiss, not a promise of things to come. He let her go and she had to force herself not to cling to him because it would be wrong to try and make him do something he didn't want to do.

'I'd better go,' he said quietly, picking up his glass from the floor beside the chair and walking over to the table to put it down. 'Did you manage to get a seat back to Sydney, by the way?'

'There's one free on a flight leaving this Friday.' She shrugged, wondering how it was possible to keep functioning when her heart was breaking. 'I should really work out my notice...'

'Don't worry about it. I'll get Dennis to sort everything out with the office.'

'Thanks. I'd appreciate it.' It was an effort to smile when it was obvious that he couldn't wait to get rid of her. Had she embarrassed him by admitting how she felt? she wondered dully as she saw him out.

Nick hadn't made any mention of how he felt about her

and she couldn't help wondering if she had misinterpreted his feelings. He had seemed upset at the thought of her being hurt, but he would have been upset for anyone in similar circumstances. Maybe he was more relieved than anything else because she would be leaving and he would no longer have to deal with the situation.

He paused on the front doorstep and Leanne steeled herself when he turned to her because she didn't want him to see how painful she found that thought.

'Thanks for being so understanding, Leanne. All I can say is that I never intended that things would get so complicated. I hope you'll try to put what has happened behind you.'

'Is that what you intend to do, Nick?' she asked, weeping inside at the thought. How could she forget him when she loved him so much?

'I'm going to try, but it isn't going to be easy.'

He touched her lightly on the cheek and her heart ached when she saw the sadness in his eyes. In that moment all her doubts disappeared and she knew that he was sending her away not because it was what he wanted but because he believed it was the right thing to do.

'Nick, please!' she began, but he didn't let her finish.

'No. There's nothing more to say, sweetheart.' Bending, he dropped a gentle kiss on her forehead and there was something so final about it that her eyes brimmed over with tears.

'Be happy, Leanne,' he whispered, before he turned and walked away.

'You, too, Nick.'

She watched him walking up the street and her heart felt like lead because there was nothing she could do to stop what was happening. She had tried her best to convince him but her best hadn't been good enough. Come Friday she would go home and try to get on with her life, but she knew that nothing would be the same ever again.

Without Nick, there would be nothing to look forward to.

* * *

The next three days were the longest of Nick's entire life and yet at the same time they were the shortest. Each day he went to work, dreading that he might not be able to stop himself telling Leanne how he really felt about her leaving. Every time he spoke to her he had to physically bite his tongue in case he poured it all out. And yet when the nights came, and he was alone in his flat, the hours seemed to fly past.

Every minute that passed was marked by the thought that it was a minute closer to her leaving. He *ached* to beg her to stay, *longed* to tell her that he loved her, but how could he? How could he ruin her life by being selfish?

Robert and Sergio had organised a farewell party for Leanne on the Thursday evening. Nick was dreading it but he couldn't think of an excuse not to attend. Fortunately, Thursday turned out to be one of their busiest days so he didn't have time to worry about it. He saw one patient after another, until he could no longer put faces to names.

Margaret and Harold Lomas called in to tell him that they were flying back to Washington that afternoon so he spent his lunch-break talking to them. Leanne had gone home and it was a relief not to have to think about her back at her flat, packing. Margaret had had keyhole surgery to remove the offending gallstones and was effusive in her praise of the treatment she had received.

Nick saw them out a short time later, thinking how good it had been to hear the outcome of the case. Once again he found himself toying with the idea of joining his father and Patrick in the family practice. His main reason for not settling down had been to avoid the risk of getting involved in a relationship, but there was no possibility of that happening now. He would never love another woman as much as he loved Leanne.

It was a depressing thought and it stayed with him for the rest of the day so that he was in no mood to celebrate when it was time for the party. He went home, fully intending to give it a miss, but the thought of not seeing her before she left was too painful.

In the end he took a cab to the bar, only to find that Leanne had already left, pleading an early start as her excuse for cutting short the evening. He stayed for a drink then went home and spent the rest of the night counting off the minutes. At seven o'clock next morning he got up and made some coffee then drank it standing by the window.

Leanne's flight would be leaving soon and she would be on her way home.

A strike by air-traffic controllers across Europe had resulted in massive delays. By the time Leanne arrived at Heathrow the queues for the check-in desks snaked all around the terminal. According to the information boards, her flight had been set back several hours and now wouldn't be leaving until midmorning.

She decided to have a cup of coffee before checking in and made her way to one of the fast-food restaurants dotted around the airport. There were long queues there as well, but she finally managed to get herself a drink. It had been too early to bother having breakfast before she had set out, but a couple of sips of the coffee were all she could manage. She felt too churned up at the thought of leaving London—and Nick.

Her eyes filled with tears and she quickly dashed them away, but it was hard to deal with the thought of never seeing him again. She should have tried harder to make him understand that they could find a solution to the problem of him not having children. She hadn't even thought to mention that they could try to adopt a child. Maybe she should go back and suggest it to him?

She sighed because in her heart she knew how pointless it would be. Nick had made up his mind and there wasn't a thing she could say that would make him change it. The best thing she could do was leave and let him get on with the life he had chosen.

* * *

Nick was on the way to his office after seeing a patient when Kim Chang waylaid him. He stopped to speak to her, hoping that she wasn't about to present him with some kind of complex problem. He'd had difficulty keeping his mind on the job that morning, understandable when his thoughts kept returning to Leanne all the time.

There was just over an hour left before her flight took off and he kept wondering if she was feeling as bad about leaving as he did about her going. The worst thing of all was knowing that he could have made her stay, but how could he have done that when he had nothing to offer her? She would be better off in Sydney with Michael.

'There's a gentleman in Reception, asking for Leanne,' Kim told him. 'I explained that she no longer worked here and he asked if he could have a word with you instead.'

'Did he say what it was about?' Nick frowned when Kim shook her head. 'I suppose I'd better speak to him, then.'

He followed her back to Reception and was surprised when he recognised Father Kenny, the young priest he had met the day that Leanne had taken him to the church in Camden.

'I'm afraid that Leanne is no longer working here,' he explained, taking the priest aside. 'She's flying home to Australia this very morning, in fact.'

'So the young lady told me.' Father Kenny sighed as he took an envelope out of his pocket and gave it to him. 'I came across this letter yesterday while I was sorting out some old papers. It's from Mary Calhoun, Leanne's mother. I recognised her name as soon as I saw the signature.'

'What on earth was it doing in the church?' Nick exclaimed.

'The adoption society which handled Leanne's case had their offices in one of the rooms attached to the parish hall,' Father Kenny explained. 'When the society closed down their records were passed to the Family Records Centre. I can only assume that this letter somehow became separated from Leanne's file. I found it in amongst a pile of old correspondence left by my predecessor.'

Nick shook his head. 'I can't believe it should have turned up now.'

'It does seem a shame.' The priest sighed. 'I was hoping to give it to Leanne, but perhaps you would be kind enough to forward it to her home address? I'm sure she would like to have it.'

'Of course. Thank you.'

Nick took the letter to his office after Father Kenny left. He sat down behind his desk and placed it on the blotter. Leanne had been desperate to find out something about the woman who had given her up for adoption and it seemed ironic that this should have turned up when she was about to fly home. Who knew if she would get another chance to come to England? This might be the only time that she was in a position to follow up the lead.

All of a sudden he knew what he had to do. He had to take the letter to her so that she could read it before she got on her plane. He checked his watch and groaned when he realised how little time remained before her flight left. Even if he took a taxi to the airport, it was doubtful if he could catch her, but he had to try. He couldn't let her leave without telling her that this letter had turned up...

He couldn't let her leave without telling her that he loved her either.

The thought slid into his head and wouldn't budge. It stayed with him while he was explaining to Robert that he had to go out and didn't disappear as he ran out of the clinic to find a taxi.

Nick told the driver to take him to Heathrow and to step on it. Whether he would be in time was debatable, but he couldn't let this last chance pass him by. He *had* to tell Leanne he loved her otherwise he would spend the rest of his life regretting it!

The queues for the check-in desks were as long as ever. Leanne shuffled along, waiting for her turn to arrive. Most of the people around her were laughing and joking, looking forward to going on holiday. With Christmas just a few weeks away, a lot of folk were flying out to Australia to visit their relatives. She felt as though she was the only one not looking forward to the trip. She was leaving Nick behind and there was no reason for her to celebrate.

There were just two people ahead of her in the queue when she heard a commotion behind her and turned round. Her eyes widened as she saw a man working his way through the crowd. Nick! What on earth was he doing there?

'I didn't think I'd make it,' he said, grinning at her, although she could see the tension that had etched deep lines either side of his mouth. 'I thought I'd get lynched for queue-jumping at one point!'

Leanne tried to think of something to say, but it was such a shock to see him there. He gave a self-conscious laugh when she remained silent.

'Don't worry, Leanne. I'm not here to cause a fuss, if that's what you're thinking. I thought you should see this before you left.' He handed her a faded white envelope.

'It's a letter from your mother,' he explained when she stared at it blankly. 'Father Kenny found it while he was sorting through some old papers. It must have fallen out of your file and that's why it wasn't with your adoption records.'

'And that's the only reason you came, Nick, is it, to give me this?'

She heard the catch in her voice and knew that he had heard it too, but there was nothing she could do about it. At one time she would have been thrilled to receive the letter, but now it meant very little to her. Nick hadn't come after her because he'd wanted to stop her leaving. He had come to deliver this letter.

It was hard to contain her anguish so that it was a moment before she realised he was speaking. She felt her heart start to pound when she heard the grating note in his voice.

'No, it isn't the only reason I came, Leanne. There was something I needed to tell you—' He broke off when the woman behind them in the queue tapped him on the shoulder and pointed out that it was their turn at the check-in desk.

Leanne saw an expression of indecision cross his face. It was obvious that he was trying to decide what to do, and all of a sudden she found herself holding her breath. Maybe it was foolish but she had a feeling that Nick might be about to tell her something she longed to hear if only he could pluck up the courage.

'I love you, Leanne. That's what I wanted to tell you.'

The words came out in a rush, as though he was afraid that he might not say them if he gave himself any time to think. Leanne felt her heart give a great bounding leap as he took hold of her hands and held onto them like a drowning man clinging to a lifeline.

'I know it isn't fair to tell you this when you're about to leave. And I'll understand if you've changed your mind about what you said the other night and don't feel the same—'

'Of course I haven't changed my mind!'

She gave a wobbly laugh when she saw the shock on his face. 'I'm crazy about you, Nick. It's been pure hell these past few days, knowing that I was leaving and that I would never see you again.'

'But are you sure? I mean, what about Michael?' he began.

'Who?' she replied, smiling at him.

'Oh, my love!'

He pulled her into his arms and kissed her soundly. It was only when they became aware that the people around them were cheering that he let her go, in fact. He grinned at her and there was a world of love in his eyes.

'I rather think we need to find some place a bit more private to continue this conversation, don't you?'

'Either that or get arrested.' She laughed up at him. 'You are sure about this, Nick Slater? I've been standing in this queue for almost an hour and I would hate to give up my place and have to start all over again. If you have any doubts, tell me now or suffer the consequences!'

'I have no doubts about how I feel, sweetheart. I just hope that I'm not being selfish—'

She kissed him quickly because she refused to let his sense of right and wrong spoil things for them. 'The only selfish thing would be to let me go home. No matter how big this problem seems at the moment, Nick, I know we can deal with it if that's what we really want.'

'It's what I want more than anything,' he told her, his voice catching.

'Then let's get out of here.'

She held out her hand, feeling her heart fill with joy when he took it. There wasn't a doubt in her mind that they were doing the right thing as they walked towards the exit. So long as they were together, they could solve any problem.

They went straight to his flat. Nick dropped her suitcase on the floor then opened his arms, feeling his heart overflow with happiness when she stepped into them. He kissed her lightly on the mouth, feeling a lump come to his throat when he saw the love in her eyes.

'I love you so much, Leanne.'

'And I love you, too,' she whispered, nestling against him.

He kissed her again, wanting her to know how much she meant to him. He had come so close to losing her that it made this moment all the more special. He sighed as he reluctantly let her go and led her into the sitting room.

'I could stand there all day just holding you, but we need to talk everything through, don't we?'

She nodded but he could see the fear in her eyes when she looked at him. 'You aren't going to have second thoughts, Nick?'

'No. I can't bear to lose you, Leanne. It's as simple as that.' He took her hand as they sat side by side on the old sofa. 'I fell in love with you the first day we met, but I was so afraid of doing the wrong thing.'

'Because of not wanting to have children?' She sighed when he nodded. 'I won't pretend that it doesn't hurt to know that I might never be able to have your baby, Nick, but it would hurt me even more if I lost you. If we can't have children of our own, we'll adopt. There are thousands of kids who need a loving home and we can give them that. There is a way round this problem—you do understand that?'

'I do now because I can't imagine living without you.' He managed a shaky smile but he was so moved by what she had said that it was hard to contain his emotions. Leanne would give up her dreams of having a family of her own so long as they could be together.

'Good, because I don't intend to let you get rid of me a second time, Nick Slater!'

He laughed as he pulled her to him and kissed her. 'So you intend to stay, do you?'

'Too right I do. I've had one close call today and I don't intend to let it happen again. Whether you like the idea or not, you're stuck with me.'

'Oh, I like it. I like it a lot...'

He couldn't continue because his mouth was too busy with more important things than speaking. He skimmed a line of kisses up her cheek to the corner of her eye, let his lips brush across her silky lashes then skate down the small, straight slope of her nose until he was right back where he had started.

This time the kiss was more intense, laced with a passion that stirred their blood. Nick held her close, making no attempt to hide how he felt. He loved her so much that he could hardly believe that he had almost lost her. Now he had been given a second chance and he didn't intend to waste it.

They made love right there on the sagging old sofa and it was so wonderful that there were tears in his eyes when it was over. Nick drew her into the crook of his arm and held her against him, knowing that he would remember this moment all his life. Being able to show Leanne how deeply he cared for her—knowing how deeply she cared for him—had touched him in a way that he could never have expected. He felt as though he'd been handed the whole world and that a lifetime of happiness was his for the taking.

In that moment, he vowed to do anything he could to make her happy, even if it meant putting aside his fears about having children. Maybe it would help if he went for counselling? So long as he could be sure that no child they had would suffer the way Matt had done, there had to be a solution. After all, there were advances being made almost daily in gene therapy, so who was to say that one day a cure might not be found? They had too much love to give a child to waste it.

He tilted her chin and looked deep into Leanne's eyes, feeling his heart swell with happiness when he saw the love in hers. 'If we found out that you aren't a carrier of Friedreich's, do you think we could maybe have a baby of our own one day?'

'Only if it's what you want, Nick. I understand your fears, really I do, and I won't ever let them come between us.' Her tone was fierce but he could see the tears in her eyes and knew how much it meant to her to hear him say that.

'I won't let that happen either,' he promised, and knew that it was a vow he would never break. No matter what happened, he wouldn't let his concerns destroy their happiness.

He kissed her again lightly but with such love that the tears poured down her face. He kissed them away and smiled at her, loving her so much that it hurt. She was everything he could have wanted and he would cherish and love her until the day he died.

'So, how soon do you think we can get married?' he asked as he settled her in his arms. He grinned when he saw the expression of shock that crossed her face.

'Married?'

'Uh-huh. That's what people do when they're in love. They go to church and stand there in front of all their family and friends and promise to love, honour and obey each other...well, the woman promises to obey, not the man. One has to sort out the ground rules, you understand.'

'Is that a fact?' One dark red eyebrow swooped towards her hairline. 'So you reckon that you're going to boss me around, do you, Dr Slater, and that I shall have to obey your every command?'

'Oh, I might allow you some freedom of choice in certain areas,' he graciously conceded. 'You can have full charge of the kitchen and all the household duties—'

He gasped as she whisked a cushion off the sofa and pelted him with it. It was quite a hard blow, hard enough to make the cushion cover split open. He laughed as a cloud of feathers exploded around them. 'Hey, you're not supposed to respond like that when a guy asks you to marry him.'

'That depends on how said guy makes his proposal!'

She sat up and glared at him. Nick felt his blood pressure rocket several dozen notches up the scale at the sight she made, sitting there stark naked in the midst of a snowy mound of feathers.

'Forget it!' She deliberately folded her arms across her chest, denying him a glimpse of her beautiful breasts. 'You'd better have a rethink, Nick Slater, or I shall be withdrawing all your conjugal rights before you've officially earned them! This marriage is going to be a partnership. Agreed?'

'Yes, fine. Anything you say,' he murmured weakly, reaching for her.

She slapped his hands away and continued to glare at him. 'Not good enough. Who knows if you might try to go back on your word in the future?'

'I won't.' He held up his hand and looked beseechingly at her. 'Scout's honour. I can't say better than that, can I?'

'I suppose not,' she conceded, grudgingly. He reached for her again but she shook her head.

'Not until you've done this properly.'

'Properly?' he repeated, wondering how long he would be able to maintain his self-control when he wanted to sweep her into his arms and make mad, passionate love to her...

He forced himself to concentrate because it seemed the quickest way to get what he really wanted. 'You mean you want me to go down on one knee and ask you to marry me?' he asked, trying not to laugh because he didn't really believe that was what she expected him to do.

'Of course. We Australian women are old-fashioned in some respects. We expect things to be done properly,' she explained with a sweet smile.

'Well, if that's what you want...' Nick shrugged as he got up from the sofa and went down on one knee. He took hold of her hand and looked at her. 'Will you do me the honour of becoming my wife, Leanne?'

'Yes, but only if you do one more thing for me.'

He felt his heart lurch when he heard how serious she sounded. 'And that is?'

'Promise me that you'll always be so gullible.' She burst out laughing. 'I never thought you'd fall for it, but it serves you right for that crack you made about me obeying you. That will teach you to toy with me, Nick Slater!'

'You wretch!'

He pulled her off the sofa, setting loose another explosion of feathers. Taking her in his arms, he kissed her soundly in loving punishment then kissed her again simply because he wanted to. He held her against his heart as a great wave of happiness swept over him and washed away the sadness that had been part of his life for far too long.

Leanne had brought love and laughter into his life. If he lived to be a hundred he would never get over how lucky he was to have found her!

CHAPTER TWELVE

IT WAS late afternoon before Leanne got round to reading the letter Father Kenny had sent her. In the hours in between she had lain in Nick's arms and they'd made plans for their future. It had been a time of healing after the pain of the past week and she knew that they'd needed it. They both knew how close they had come to losing one another and that made what they had all the more special and to be cherished.

Nick got up and switched on the light then went to the bedroom and came back with his dressing-gown for her to wear. 'I'm going to take a shower while you read your letter.'

He bent and kissed her and she could see the love in his eyes. 'I'm here if you need me, sweetheart, but I think you need to do this on your own. OK?'

'OK,' she whispered, loving him for understanding how she felt. She picked up the letter after he had left the room and stared at it for a long time. She had pinned her hopes on finding out about the woman who had given birth to her but all of a sudden she was terrified of what she might discover. In the end, she summoned up her courage and ripped open the envelope, her eyes filling with tears as she read what Mary Calhoun had written all those years ago.

'Are you all right?'

She looked up when she heard the concern in Nick's voice as he came back from taking his shower. 'Yes, I'm fine. It's just so moving...' She had to swallow the lump in her throat.

Nick sat down beside her and gathered her into his arms. 'Why couldn't she keep you, Leanne?' he asked softly, his warm breath stirring the hair at her temple, his hand stroking lightly up and down her arm.

'Because she was afraid that she wouldn't be able to look after me properly.'

She stared at the letter, trying to imagine how Mary must have felt when she had written it. There was so much love in the carefully written lines and it was unbearably moving to imagine the heartache Mary must have suffered.

'Does she say anything about your father?' he prompted.

'Yes.' She swallowed again. 'She met him while she was on holiday in Venice and they fell in love. He was married and he told her that he could never leave his wife because it would break her heart. They had just two weeks together and she never saw him again. When she found out she was pregnant, she decided that it would be wrong to tell him.'

'That must have been a difficult decision for her.' He held her close for a moment. 'How old was she when she had you? Just a teenager?'

'No. She was forty-four and had never been married. She was a teacher at a tiny village school in Ireland.' She shook her head. 'It must have been so hard for her, Nick. Can you imagine how people would have gossiped if they had found out she was pregnant? That's why she took leave of absence and came to England to have me.'

'And it's why she made the decision to have you adopted. She wanted you to have a family who would love and care for you the way she could never do.'

'Yes.' Tears ran down Leanne's face. 'She says that she loved me too much to be selfish and keep me. If people had found out that she'd had an illegitimate child, she would have been forced to give up her job and would have had no way to support us. She was also worried because of her age. She felt it would be better if I had someone to look after me who would be around to watch me growing up.'

'It can't have been easy for her to make those decisions, Leanne, but she did what she thought was right. I know how difficult it can be to do that.'

She heard the ache in his voice and turned to him. 'It's always hard when you put other people first. That's what makes you and Mary so special. I can't begin to tell you how much it means to me to read this letter. Thank you for bringing it to me.'

'I think it's Mary we should be thanking because if it hadn't been for her letter, you might be on your way back to Australia by now.' He kissed her gently. 'I shall always be grateful to her for that. I only wish I could tell her.'

'Maybe you can.' She gave him the letter and pointed to the address at the top. 'She put her address on it, Nick. She wouldn't have done that it she hadn't wanted me to find her, would she?'

'Then that's what you must do.' He turned her to face him. 'We shall find out if she's still living at that address and go to see her, if that's what you want, Leanne.'

'It is,' she whispered, then said nothing else because Nick was kissing her again.

She wrapped her arms around him as a feeling of peace enveloped her. She had found out about the woman who had given birth to her and she had found Nick. Coming to England had been the best decision she had ever made!

Four months later...

The tiny village church was packed. Penny had thrown herself into the preparations with all the fervour of the newly-wed. Nick knew that they couldn't have hoped to get everything organised in time if it hadn't been for his sister's help.

Life had been hectic for the past few months, hectic but so wonderful that many times he'd had to pinch himself to make sure he wasn't dreaming. He had returned to Sussex after his contract at the clinic had ended and had joined his father and Patrick at the family practice. Leanne had moved there with him and they had found a cottage in the village which they were in the process of decorating.

At his father's suggestion, she had taken the job as their new practice nurse so not only did he see her at home each night, he had the pleasure of working with her each day. Nick knew that his family loved her almost as much as he did and it made him intensely happy to see how quickly she had settled in. Family mattered, as he had discovered.

Leanne had been for tests and last week they'd received confirmation that she wasn't a carrier of Friedeich's ataxia. It had been a relief for them both, although Nick knew in his heart that they would have handled the news if it hadn't been so positive. They could deal with anything so long as they did it together.

He had attended several counselling sessions and it had helped enormously to discuss his fears with other people who were carriers of an inherited genetic disorder. So many had been faced with the same difficult choices as he had been.

The organist began to play the opening bars of the Wedding March. Nick took a deep breath and stood up. He turned to face the door so that he could watch Leanne coming down the aisle on her father's arm. His gaze skimmed over his family in the pew behind him and he smiled as he saw the delight on their faces. They were so pleased that he had found happiness at last.

His gaze moved on to the slender, white-haired woman in the front pew to his right, and they exchanged a look that spoke volumes about how they both felt on this very special occasion. He and Leanne had found Mary Calhoun living at the address she had given in her letter. She had never married, neither had she had any more children. She had lived in the village where she had taught in the hope that one day the daughter she had given up would try to find her.

Nick knew that he would never forget the day he and Leanne had gone to see Mary for the first time. Watching her meeting the woman who had given birth to her had touched his heart. He could feel tears in his eyes even now when he thought about it but, then, he was already feeling emotional. Was it any wonder when his dream was about to come true?

He looked towards the aisle and his breath caught when he got his first glimpse of Leanne. She looked so beautiful in the long, white dress, so regal as she walked proudly towards him. She was carrying a bouquet of spring flowers and there were more flowers in her hair. She had decided not to wear a veil and he could see her smiling as she walked towards him.

He stepped out of the pew and went to meet her, uncaring what the congregation thought as he bent and kissed her softly on the mouth. Maybe he was supposed to wait until *after* the ceremony before he kissed his bride, but he didn't care. He loved her so much and he wanted the whole world to know that in a short time she would be his for ever.

He led her to the altar, held her hand, felt her fingers gripping his as the vicar began the service. He could feel the love that flowed between them and his heart swelled with joy as they stood together at the altar and made their vows.

For better, for worse.
In sickness and in health.
For richer, for poorer.

Nick repeated the promises and meant them with every scrap of his being. He would always love Leanne and one day, in the not too distant future, they would come back to this church together and watch their child being christened.

One day.

Soon.

Modern Romance™
...seduction and
passion guaranteed

Tender Romance™
...love affairs that
last a lifetime

Sensual Romance™
...sassy, sexy and
seductive

Blaze
...sultry days and
steamy nights

Medical Romance™
...medical drama on
the pulse

Historical Romance™
...rich, vivid and
passionate

27 new titles every month.

*With all kinds of Romance for
every kind of mood...*

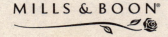

MILLS & BOON

Medical Romance™

MORE THAN CARING by Josie Metcalfe

Lauren Scott has never found it easy to invest in relationships – instead she's invested her care in nursing her patients. Then handsome hospital administrator Marc Fletcher comes to her rescue and it seems Lauren has finally found a man she can trust. But Marc has also been running away from relationships and, if they are to have a chance together, Lauren must persuade Marc to accept some TLC in return.

HER UNEXPECTED FAMILY by Gill Sanderson

When Nurse Tessa Calvert helped a troubled woman on her radio show it turned out to be the rebellious young daughter of her new boss, A&E consultant James Armstrong – and he was furious at Tessa's inappropriate advice! Despite their explosive beginning, both James and Tessa soon felt the powerful attraction emerging between them…

THE VISITING SURGEON by Lucy Clark

Surgeon Susie Monahan has no intention of acting on the instant attraction between herself and gorgeous visiting orthopaedic professor Jackson Myers. She's been badly hurt before – and he's only in Brisbane for a week. Despite her fears, she finds herself longing to hold him in her arms and never let him go!

On sale 4th October 2002

Available at most branches of WH Smith, Tesco, Martins, Borders, Eason, Sainsbury's and all good paperback bookshops.

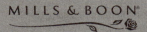

Medical Romance™

THE DOCTOR'S RUNAWAY BRIDE
by Sarah Morgan

Moments before her wedding, midwife Tia Franklin knew she couldn't marry Dr Luca Zattoni. She'd made a discovery about him that had shattered her dreams, so she left Venice – and the man she loved. But Luca followed her to England. This passionate Italian fully intended to claim his bride – *and* their unborn child…

ACCIDENTAL REUNION *by Carol Marinelli*

Dr Declan Haversham hasn't seen Lila Bailey since she left him standing at a bus stop in his boxer shorts eight years ago! Now Lila has become a successful emergency nurse, though Declan once laughed at the idea. He knows she is still angry with him – how can he persuade her to give him one last chance to make their dreams come true?

THE BACHELOR DOCTOR *by Judy Campbell*

Jake Donahue is a fantastic doctor – and incredibly sexy too! He has no time for commitment or marriage, but his world is thrown upside-down when Dr Cara Mackenzie breezes back into his life. When emergency after emergency flings Jake and Cara together, Jake finds himself being seriously tempted out of bachelorhood…

On sale 4th October 2002

Available at most branches of WH Smith, Tesco, Martins, Borders, Eason, Sainsbury's and all good paperback bookshops.

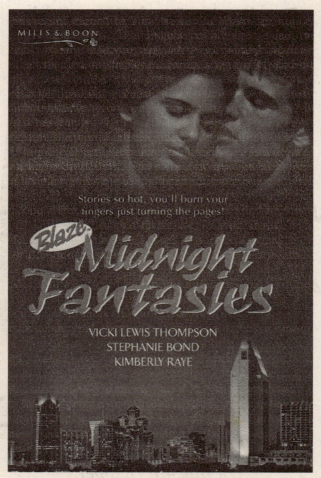

Don't miss *Book Two* of this BRAND-NEW 12 book collection 'Bachelor Auction'.

Who says money can't buy love?

On sale 4th October

Available at most branches of WH Smith, Tesco, Martins, Borders, Eason, Sainsbury's, and all good paperback bookshops.

FREE
2 BOOKS
AND A SURPRISE GIFT!

We would like to take this opportunity to thank you for reading this Mills & Boon® book by offering you the chance to take TWO more specially selected titles from the Medical Romance™ series absolutely FREE! We're also making this offer to introduce you to the benefits of the Reader Service™—

- ★ FREE home delivery
- ★ FREE monthly Newsletter
- ★ FREE gifts and competitions
- ★ Exclusive Reader Service discount
- ★ Books available before they're in the shops

Accepting these FREE books and gift places you under no obligation to buy; you may cancel at any time, even after receiving your free shipment. Simply complete your details below and return the entire page to the address below. ***You don't even need a stamp!***

YES! Please send me 2 free Medical Romance books and a surprise gift. I understand that unless you hear from me, I will receive 4 superb new titles every month for just £2.55 each, postage and packing free. I am under no obligation to purchase any books and may cancel my subscription at any time. The free books and gift will be mine to keep in any case.

M2ZEC

Ms/Mrs/Miss/Mr ....Initials ....
BLOCK CAPITALS PLEASE

Surname ....

Address ....

....

....Postcode ....

Send this whole page to:
UK: FREEPOST CN81, Croydon, CR9 3WZ
EIRE: PO Box 4546, Kilcock, County Kildare (stamp required)

Offer valid in UK and Eire only and not available to current Reader Service subscribers to this series. We reserve the right to refuse an application and applicants must be aged 18 years or over. Only one application per household. Terms and prices subject to change without notice. Offer expires 31st December 2002. As a result of this application, you may receive offers from other carefully selected companies. If you would prefer not to share in this opportunity please write to The Data Manager at the address above.

Mills & Boon® is a registered trademark owned by Harlequin Mills & Boon Limited.
Medical Romance™ is being used as a trademark.